———————— ★ ————————

HE DIDN'T TRUST COINCIDENCES. THEY SMACKED TOO MUCH OF GODS ABOVE PULLING STRINGS....

Yet this girl—for Kemp was certain now that it could be no other—had come to Crownberry Avenue on Sunday, May 7, and cheekily appropriated Malcolm Moss from under the eyes of his wife. On Friday night, May 12, Lennox Kemp, submerged in flowers, had watched two men struggling with a burden in the boot of Moss's car.

It didn't take a genius to work it out: the burden had been the body of Lucille Pearson. Any heavy-footed detective could have reached that conclusion without damaging his cerebellum. The question Kemp had to answer was: what was he going to do about it?

———————— ★ ————————

"A neatly plotted story full of surprises."

—*Rocky Mountain News*

"Typical of the best kind of English mystery."

—*The Practical Lawyer*

Hang the CONSEQUENCES

M.R.D. MEEK

WORLDWIDE.®

TORONTO • NEW YORK • LONDON • PARIS
AMSTERDAM • STOCKHOLM • HAMBURG
ATHENS • MILAN • TOKYO • SYDNEY

HANG THE CONSEQUENCES

A Worldwide Mystery/November 1988

This edition is reprinted by arrangement with
Charles Scribner's Sons, an Imprint of Macmillan
Publishing Company.

ISBN 0-373-26011-3

Hang the
CONSEQUENCES

PROLOGUE—1938

'THE LAD'LL SURELY not go to school today?' The man's voice was hesitant, embarrassed.

She crossed the kitchen and tilted the kettle from the hob to heat the brown earthenware teapot.

'He'll go to the school like any other day.' She went briskly to empty the hot water at the sink as she answered. More perceptive than he yet inhibited by complex emotions to which she could give no name, she took comfort in the small everyday actions.

The man sighed. He seated himself at the plain scrubbed table for his breakfast as he had always done in some twenty years of well-ordered life.

'Aye,' he said, 'you're maybe right there.' In all those years he had found it inexorably to be so.

But the present circumstances blurred even his certainty as to her judgement. He took his plate from her hands and ventured into that doubt.

'Are we to say nothing to him, then?'

She stood, for once at a loss, despite the surety of domestic routine, her fingers twisting at the threads inside her apron pockets.

'What else can we do? How can we talk about it? He's not ten yet. How would we find the words? I just wouldn't know what to say...'

The silence that followed was gently edged away in the splutter of frying bacon, and the sound and the aroma somehow consoled them both.

'I've cooked him a bit extra,' she said, taking refuge within her own scope, 'he doesn't seem to eat near enough.'

'Well,' he said, 'it stands to reason. He's had a lot to put up with of late.'

'Ssh . . . Here he comes.'

There was only a strip of linoleum on the stairs. She had heard the clump of young feet, certain and loud.

'Your bacon's on the stove. Come on, lad, get your breakfast into you,' she called to him, bustling about, glad to have things to do.

The boy came in, slowly at first, then, finding the scene looked normal, with greater assurance. He wore black boots, short grey flannel trousers, grey shirt, grey jumper and a navy school blazer. His grey and red knitted tie was a bit askew, the knot perhaps nervously pulled too tight.

'Sleep well, did you, lad?' said the man, glancing up from the table but without too obvious a scrutiny.

'Yes, thank you.' He hitched his small boot heels on to the spar of the kitchen chair. He wished he had shoes rather than boots. Most of the other boys had shoes for school, not just for best.

'I've cooked you an extra piece of bacon,' she said, leaning over him and putting down his breakfast. 'I know you like a nice piece of bacon.' She turned away abruptly and busied herself with the teapot. 'And there's a nice cup of tea for you. It's a cold morning.'

The fire crackled, and ashes fell softly through the grate with faint puffing sounds as the boy ate his breakfast. No words were spoken. Grey light outside slowly grew, enlarging the window-pane.

'Got everything ready for school, then?' she said at last, putting off her apron and bringing her own cup to the table.

'Yes,' said the boy, 'I'll just get my satchel.'

He closed the door quietly and they listened to the clatter of boots on the stairs.

'I'll be off to my work.' The man took his coat and cap from the peg and put them on. He opened the back door to the yard where he kept his bicycle. Then, still turning matters over in his mind, he came back.

'We must use yon things on the mantelpiece if it comes to it,' he said.

She followed his reluctant glance, and looked at the dirty canvas bag lying among the brass ornaments and everyday clutter.

'If it's necessary, aye,' she said nervously, 'but I'll not touch them. She left a bit of money in the Post Office—I'll not mind using that. But them—no, I won't touch them. He can have them some day, then it'll be no concern of ours. But in the meantime, can't we manage without them?' There was appeal in her eyes.

The man knew that for once the decision was his. Too much had already been put upon her. In a moment of rare insight he realized that there was perhaps a limit. It came to him that a very long time ago in an almost forgotten war he had had to take such decisions.

He went across the kitchen and put an arm round her shoulders. It was an unusual gesture. For all their great contentment in one another they seldom touched, save in the privacy of the double bed upstairs they'd shared since the day he'd come back from Flanders.

She put her hand up and closed it instinctively over his fingers gripping her shoulders. 'It's all right,' he said, 'we'll not touch them, we can manage without. Put them away somewhere so they'll be forgotten till the time comes he's grown up and he'll know what to do.'

She nodded, not trusting herself to speak, but she smiled for the first time that morning. 'Off you go now, or you'll be late for your work. And never mind what your mates have to say...'

When the boy came in again, trailing his satchel, she had his lunch-box ready. 'There's your piece,' she said, 'and I've put an apple in.'

He stowed it away in his satchel and turned to the door, pulling at his woollen scarf.

'Don't forget to call in at Mr Crockett's on the way home to get your good shoes—he'll have mended the soles by now. They're all paid for. 'Bye, then, lad.'

'Goodbye...' The boy didn't know yet what he was to call her, so, like any other boy, he hid behind that ignorance and said nothing. He reached up for the high latch and let himself out into the street.

HE CAME HOME from school as he usually did just after four o'clock. There was a warm cosy smell of baking scones. He put his satchel carefully down in a corner, and handed the woman the pair of shoes from the menders. She scrutinized them.

'These'll do fine,' she said grudgingly, 'but he might have put a bit paper round them. Away you go now and wash your hands. Your tea's ready.'

He enjoyed his scones and plum jam, and asked for more of the damp fruit cake she brought out of a special tin for him. Despite appearance to the contrary, he was a good eater.

She sat and talked to him as they both drank the hot sweet tea. She asked him about school, and he answered as he thought she should be answered.

He did not tell her that, for him, it had been a strange sort of day. His class teacher, who didn't usually pay him much attention except to say, 'Sit up straight and pay attention,' had that morning helped him with his sums. She had put a hand on his shoulder as she explained where he had gone wrong, and for once the touch of that bony hand was gentle. On the stairs at break two of the bigger boys had him cornered with his back against the cold brown tiles, their impudent eyes bright and threatening. Immediately the awesome figure of the headmaster, rarely seen and consequently feared by all, was at his side and the two louts had melted away. Nothing had been said. At home time, as the children poured out, the teacher who stood by the railings to see that the road was clear of traffic had come over to him.

'Will you be all right going home?' she asked.

'Yes, I'm all right,' he had answered, and wondered. He didn't live far from the school and other children had much more difficult journeys than he.

All these things he kept to himself because they were strange and he wanted time to think about them.

Later that night he took his satchel upstairs with him when he went to bed.

He slept in the little spare room at the back of the house. It was bare and rather cold but some effort had been made to make it comfortable for him. There was a rag rug on the floor beside the bed and another by the table near the window, and on the table he had the luxury of a silk-shaded lamp which gave a good light. He remembered that lamp from another time and how he used to peer under it and marvel at its silken glow.

Methodically and without haste the boy undid the straps of his satchel and took out a crumpled piece of newspaper.

It was a Special—the midday edition. He had watched Mr Crockett pick it up off the counter to wrap the mended shoes in, and he'd seen the name in the headline at precisely the same time as Mr Crockett had also seen it. The old shoe-repairer's hands stopped moving suddenly and he stared at the boy, his face slowly reddening. But the boy calmly held out his hands for the parcel, knowing without a doubt that if he didn't take it immediately Mr Crockett would tear the paper off. He wanted to run from the shop, but somehow with an effort of will he walked out, closing the door with a deliberate click as if to shut off the sight of the man's embarrassment.

Now he spread the newspaper carefully on the table-top and smoothed out the creases. He pulled up the plain wooden chair, adjusted the lamp and, with his elbows on the table and his chin on his hands, he began to read.

Down one side of the page ran the newsprint under the great black heading; on the other was a picture taken outside the gaol that morning—in the grey light of dawn, said the print. The cobblestones were wet and shining with rain.

The boy read on. Although he did not know the word, the description was graphic. As he read so he could see: the prison warders going about their duties, the presence of the Governor and the Chaplain, the steady tramp of feet on stone corridors, the room itself, the trapdoor, the shadow of the rope, and the shabby figure in the middle of all the ritual. Then the pinioning, the hooding, the adjustment at the neck, and finally, the clanging thud and the swinging man.

The boy read on.

There had been a small crowd at the prison gate. Some lady, she had a foreign name, had made a protest, there were long words which he read syllable by syllable without understanding—'abolition of capital punishment'... In his mind there arose a vague picture of Romans in togas turning down their thumbs.

But the newspaper had told it plain enough; the notice had gone up outside the prison. The boy read on, and now he knew why that day had been different.

His father had been hanged by the neck until he was dead.

ONE

LENNOX KEMP STARED glumly out through the dusty window of McCready's Detective Agency and wondered, not for the first time, why he had become so attached to the place. It could hardly be the surroundings—Beaver Lane, Walthamstow, wasn't Baker Street, and 110 was seedy red-brick above the dry cleaner's, not an old brownstone on West Thirty-fifth. Nor could the tide of business which flowed intermittently through its doors be other than the backwash of suburban divorce, the humdrum service of repugnant writs, and the scavenger hunt through the debris of disordered lives left shipwrecked by intricacies in Court orders.

Although McCready himself might like to identify his operatives with the late Philip Marlowe or Lew Archer, missing heiresses were rare around Finsbury Park; there wasn't even much high-class skulduggery at local bingo halls—certainly not up to the standards of Las Vegas—and Kemp had long given up any such illusions.

Yet he stayed on, even now when he had the chance to escape, the chance to return once more to the respectable trade from which he had been ousted some six years previously. Why on earth did he hesitate, he thought, meeting the calm gaze of the pale-haired girl in the Harp lager poster on the hoarding opposite. Perhaps you have a penchant for low life, she seemed to be telling him, perhaps you prefer the underside of things and have no taste for the sunny uplands. Perhaps I have no sense of class, he told himself gloomily, turning from the window when Elvira brought in his coffee.

Now Elvira knew all about class—and prized it highly. Class was talking refined on the phone, rounding her East End vowels, having what she called client-contact, wearing dark office clothes with pure white trim, and not carrying your shopping in a string-bag. For all her affectations, which were many and trying, Elvira was a demon typist, manic, fast and accurate. She could calculate in her head like a French peasant and although the Agency might have preferred a more fun-loving maid of all work it was worth putting up with her irritating niceness if only to get the accounts balanced. Her attitude to the more unsavoury aspects of the work was ambivalent; something between hauteur and there-but-for-the-grace-of-God, as if she feared that only a well-shod foot was keeping her out of the mire. So that when she rang through to tell Lennox Kemp that there was a Mrs Moss in reception he sensed both disapproval and divorce in her voice.

As he could not afford to be so dainty in his choice of clients, he said he'd be right out, thinking wearily that here was yet another piece of flotsam to be salvaged.

He walked down the short dark corridor to the cubbyhole which housed Elvira's fortunately meagre body, the filing cabinets, the ramshackle safe, and her typewriter desk, where, on a strip of worn carpet waiting clients drummed their anxious heels, and collected his Mrs Moss.

On first impression she made little impact but Kemp had long given up expecting either Brigid O'Shaughnessy or Pussy Galore, just as he had also abandoned the idea of ever becoming the Perry Mason of the Central Criminal Court.

In his own room, where the early May sunlight was winning a stealthy battle against the dust, Mrs Moss became a person of thirty or so, maybe older but worn well, or younger but tired, wrapped in a large tweed coat as an envelope rather than in any concession to fashion or cost, so that she had no figure, good or bad, and with her legs drawn back into the shadow under her chair, Kemp had no guide as to their shapeliness or otherwise. Not that he judged female clients solely on their looks, but first impressions do make lasting images, and he had found that women give an outward representation of themselves by the manner of their dress more accurately approximating to their real personalities than they suppose.

He took down the basic data of name and address, which she gave clearly enough but in a voice devoid of accent. Her face was well-shaped, pale-skinned, smudged darkish under brown eyes which were not themselves dark. She wore a small-brimmed felt or velour hat of the kind which used to be worn equally by ladies choosing tea in Fortnum's and local house-wives buying cabbage in Walthamstow market. But in these, the free-wheeling days of the Sixties, any hat was an anachronism.

No clues then as to background either in appearance or voice. Kemp began to attend to his notes.

'Frances Jessica Moss, married.' Nice name.

'Seventy-two, Crownberry Avenue.' Local. But not so very local. Not City, nor exactly suburban. What had been in Victorian and Edwardian times, and increasingly so since, the hinterland. Now very difficult to judge whether it had declined, or having gone down in the world might be on the up-and-up. Large houses hiding behind laurelled shrubberies, low broken walls with the socket holes still showing where metal railings had gone for the war effort; sudden luxurious upsurges of glass and concrete where developer-demolishers had struck lucky and turned them into bonanzas, the gold bricks of modern flats; tall old houses with peeling plaster where the variations in curtains floor to floor and even from window to window indicated the social decline into bedsitters. A difficult address to evaluate. Carry on, Mrs Moss.

She got to the nub faster than he thought she would. Most women dodged round it—like straightening the covers on the settee. Men were invariably quicker, being used to the practical application of the fallacy that time is money, and being firmly trained by employers, solicitors and accountants to be aware of the meter ticking up the cost of temporary hiring of an expert mind.

'My husband has disappeared and I want you to find him.'

'How long has he been gone?'

'He left home last Sunday evening about eight o'clock. This is Friday, so that makes it nearly five days.'

'This is unusual?'

'He's never done anything like this before, but then the whole thing is so unbelievable...' She let slip the shadow of a smile. 'You see, he left with this girl...'

If Kemp had felt even a flicker of interest it quickly faded. The old, old story.

'How long has he known the girl?'

'I don't know. I don't know anything. It all happened very fast—there wasn't time to find out anything. Let me tell you in as proper order as I can make it.' She paused, thinking backwards.

'I suppose I should have known there was something wrong. He hasn't been well lately, which in itself is unusual. He is normally very healthy. I thought he had been overworking but work suits Malcolm. He certainly had been coming home later and later...' She was looking in her mind at uncomfortable facts that were possibly new to her. But not to Kemp. He only hoped that boredom would not show in his face so he looked out of the window and again met the gaze of the Harp girl. Oh, you hussy, he thought. The oldest tale in the world. Far on the ringing plains of windy Troy.

Mrs Moss's small, even voice continued.

'He was in on Sunday evening when the telephone went but I answered it as I was in the hall. All the voice at the other end said was: "I'm ready—it's time for us to go." I said: "What? Who do you want?"—the sort of thing one says when they've got the wrong number. But the odd thing was that nothing was said at the other end. No sorry or anything, yet they didn't ring off, so I put the receiver back. When I looked up Malcolm was standing half way up the stair looking at me in such a peculiar way that I said: "What's wrong?" He didn't answer so I said: "Someone was on the phone. It was a girl's voice, she said something about it being time to go, then she didn't say any more." Malcolm just seemed to collapse. He fell on the stairs and when I reached him he was in a kind of faint.'

Kemp interrupted.

'Was the call from a phone-box?'

She looked startled. He had broken in on a narrative in which she was reliving an experience as one would concentrate to recall a dream on waking.

'It must have been. I remember the pips going when I picked up the phone. Afterwards I thought it must have been quite close. Well, afterwards I knew it had been very close.' She stopped.

'Malcolm was out for perhaps two or three minutes, then he recovered. I helped him upstairs and he lay down on top of the quilt in our bedroom.'

Well, at least they didn't have separate bedrooms. Kemp was trying to remember his small store of U and non-U adages—who says quilt and who says eiderdown. He gave up and wondered if he could get her round to mirror and looking-glass. He was aware his mind was wandering, and he began to be as much irritated by his inability to place her as he was with his own obsession with the nuances of social class.

'I asked Malcolm if he had hurt himself when he fell and he said, no, he was all right but he would like a hot drink. I was in the kitchen making some coffee when the front doorbell rang and I answered it. There was this girl. She walked right in past me...' Mrs Moss gave a little helpless gesture as she might also have done at the time. 'It was all happening so fast—and yet I knew it was the same person who had spoken on the phone. She said: "Where's Malcolm?" It seemed such an ordinary inquiry, such as any visitor to the house might make, so I just said, "He's upstairs lying down, he's not very well"... Then she was going for the stairs very quickly calling his name. I heard him answer her and she went straight into the bedroom and they closed the door, and I could hear them talking. I could hear them talking... and the coffee percolator bubbling in the kitchen...' She broke off. Kemp waited for her to go on, watching her.

She seemed surprisingly relaxed. Most women by now would have been successfully or unsuccessfully, depending on their temperament, fighting the rising hysteria.

'I made the coffee. Isn't it odd that when one is so shocked that one doesn't know what to do one does the most normal of things, doesn't one?'

'One does.' That had been a lot of 'ones', and even as Kemp made the comment there was a sudden flicker of appraisal in the light brown eyes, and he realized that assessment can be a two-way game.

'Then I heard them both coming downstairs. Malcolm had his overcoat on and was carrying his suitcase.'

So far Frances Jessica Moss had told her story with remarkable precision. It was only now that she appeared discomposed. Her pallor increased.

'Mrs Moss, would you like a cup of tea?' She nodded, and Kemp pressed his buzzer for Elvira and asked for some tea. When it came Mrs Moss thanked Elvira with a warm smile and an equanimity which surprised Kemp and drew from Elvira an unexpected gesture of sympathy. Well then, thought Kemp, no tears. And a demeanour which smacked of that instinctive rightness of attitude to servants which betokened an acceptance of their presence possibly since childhood.

'This girl, Mrs Moss. I gather she was a complete stranger to you. What was she like?'

'She was very good-looking. Young, blonde . . . I'd never seen her before, and yet . . . Oh, I know who she reminded me of . . . That advertisement for somebody's lager.'

Kemp couldn't help a glance out of the window. But of course she wasn't just his poster—they were everywhere that year.

'What happened next?'

She looked back absently into her mind and her recollection, and Kemp suddenly thought: She's rerunning the film.

'They both went into the sitting-room.' The sitting-room, Kemp noted, not the lounge. 'And they just stood there when I followed them. There were the three of us standing there looking at each other. You know, like a still from a film . . .'

Kemp saw again that flicker of something sharp in her eyes and felt the sense of an intrusion into his own thought process.

'Then what?'

'Well, it was the girl who did most of the talking, Malcolm said very little . . . Oh, except when he said quite clearly and distinctly that he was going away with . . . but even then he never said her name . . .'

Mrs Moss looked down at the soft kid gloves which she kept folding and unfolding in her lap. Kid gloves in Beaver Lane? Kemp almost felt like laughing until he saw the flash of two rings, one safely bedded down below the matrimonial band on the left, the other sparkling a brilliant green when it caught the sun. His mind slid away into the question of costs.

'The girl talked to me in a soothing kind of voice, but very firm. Like a nurse. She said that Malcolm and she had fallen in love and were going away together, and that as there were no children to be considered it would only be me who would be hurt and they were both very sorry...'

She trailed off into silence. She seemed puzzled by what she had said. 'It all sounds like a magazine story but perhaps that's how things really are said. There were a lot of banalities somehow. I remember I thought so at the time. Funny how one can think like that at a time like that.' She even laughed a little and threw Kemp another of those curiously perceptive glances. He felt he was being thrown a thin gold lassoo, and tenuous though the feeling was, he was disturbed. Was she having him on? He didn't like the idea of the thin gold noose so he threw her back something more solid and did it with more force than he normally would have used.

'Finding your husband might be costly, Mrs Moss, and in any case, even if we do find him, from what they both said to you—and you're the best judge of that—he won't come back. Do you just want his address for the service of divorce papers or do you want to take out a summons for a maintenance order?'

She stared at him for a moment without speaking, but if he had hoped to rattle her with his bedrock approach her calm eyes showed no sign of it.

'I've already seen a solicitor. I hardly know him except that he handles all Malcolm's business, building contracts, that sort of thing. It was Mr Clement Fawcett who suggested your Agency—reluctantly, I'm afraid...'

I'll bet, thought Kemp; Fawcett's was a highly respectable firm who would only resort to employing McCready's if they were pushed.

As if echoing his mind, she went on: '...but only because he thought I ought to wait.'

'What about the police?'

'No,' she said, with certain finality.

Kemp shrugged. 'You're probably right. I don't suppose they'd be interested in a missing husband—particularly when he went off deliberately with a young girl.'

Her colour rose.

'Are you interested, Mr Kemp?' she asked steadily.

Touché. He had to admit she had nettled him, so his tone was rough.

'Yes, if you are willing to pay. We are no part of the Welfare State.' It was a favorite maxim of McCready's.

She laughed. It was an unexpected and surprisingly pleasant sound.

'I have no money,' she said, and seemed almost to savour his astonishment. 'When my husband left he took his cheque-book and anyway the bank account is in his name, and there was very little cash in the house. It too is in Malcolm's name but I understand I have the right to remain there, and that is being taken care of by Mr Fawcett. And he's getting in touch with the bank . . .'

Kemp sat back and cross-hatched the doodles on his notepad. 'Inquiries do cost money, Mrs Moss. If, as you say, you've been to Fawcett's you will know you can get legal aid which might stretch to the expense of eventually tracing your husband. But if you come to our Agency privately, as you have done, then you will have to pay us. Why not leave it entirely in the hands of your solicitor?'

'Because I just won't wait, Mr Kemp. I don't want a divorce, I don't want a maintenance order. I simply want to know where my husband is and if he's all right. Look, Mr Kemp—' she made a sudden movement—'I've said I've no money to pay you at the moment but I do have this.'

She raised her hand and Kemp saw what had flashed green.

If it was real then it was a huge emerald, and from the fire in its depths there was no doubt that it was real. It would pay the rent of 110 Beaver Lane for more years than the lease had to run.

She must have seen the shock in his face because she drew the ring from her finger, put it on the desk and pushed it towards him.

'I mean it,' she said, 'you can sell it for me.' She said it quite seriously as though it were quite in the normal course of business for McCready's to be offered jewellery in lieu of fees. Something of her earnestness communicated itself to him, so he decided to go along with it.

He bent down to his desk drawer and took out a plain sheet of quarto and wrote, dictating as he did so:

'I, Frances Jessica Moss, have handed to Lennox Kemp my gold ring with the square emerald set in diamonds and—' he turned it to the light and looked inside—'marked M.M. to F.J.M. 1961, on condition that he sell it on my behalf and from the proceeds thereof deduct his fees for work which I have this day engaged him to do, before accounting to me for the residue.'

He handed her a pen and she signed the paper: F. Jessica Moss. It was the best he could do in the circumstances; he just hoped to God he'd covered himself—although he could already hear prosecuting Counsel's amused disbelief: 'Surely, Mr Kemp, you do not normally accept your costs in emeralds? I should not have thought in your line of—er—business your retainer for finding a missing husband would run to that sort of figure!'

Kemp took up the paper, dated it, put it in an envelope with the ring and stuck it in a corner of his blotter. Then he went back to his notes.

'Now, Mrs Moss, I shall need to know more about your husband. What does he do?'

'He's an architect. I suppose he's very successful. There has always been plenty of money, although neither of us is very extravagant—oh, except—' she had the grace to blush—'he did give me jewellery on my birthdays. I'm afraid I know very little about his business, or about his financial matters.'

Kemp went on with his questions for another thirty minutes, and at the end of that time could piece together a picture of their marriage as flat as a painting done by a child, with no shading, no tone, a simple outline without substance.

They had met at a tennis party at her mother's house in Folkestone when Frances Jessica was on holiday from her boarding-school and married two years later in the local church with a reception in the grounds of that house—it all sounded very pat, and slotted Mrs Moss nicely into an acceptable social background. But to Kemp's probing mind there was yet something hazy and nostalgic about it; girls in white tennis dresses, ladies gathering roses in baskets, shady trees and tea on the lawn, and young men standing about in blazers—like a scene shot through a veil by an *avant garde* film director. Perhaps it was his imagination, perhaps it was the way she told it, perhaps a subconscious yearning on his own part—it was all so totally at variance with the dreary offices of the Agency above the dry cleaner's, the newsagent's across the way with cards in the fly-blown window advertising cheap rooms and second-hand bicycles, where the town development plan had stopped and turned aside in despair because the area really wasn't worth the bother.

Malcolm Moss had evidently been doing pretty well when he married Jessica. The house in Crownberry

Avenue had been bought at that time and although recently he had talked vaguely about buying elsewhere, they had never moved. He had been a partner in a firm called Archer & Co. in Islington but old Mr Archer had since died and Malcolm carried on the firm himself with a small staff. Their offices were apparently still at Islington with a branch at Loughton.

'You realize that I shall have to see your husband's associates?' said Kemp at that point. 'Do they know that he's missing?'

'Not yet. Mr Fawcett advised against telling them—for the time being. He suggested I say that Malcolm is ill, or has gone on holiday. He hasn't been in to the office since last Friday. Mr. Fawcett got one of his staff to telephone... It wasn't something I could do.'

It was clear that Mrs Moss took no interest in her husband's business. Whether this was due to inertia on her part, or whether Malcolm Moss believed in placing people in their rightful niche and keeping them there, was hard to determine. Kemp had already gained the impression of an exact man, serious so far as his profession was concerned, a quiet-living man. Still waters however don't necessarily run to great depths, they are often merely stagnant. Not that in Mrs Moss's narrative there had appeared any criticism of her husband; on the contrary, she had been scrupulous in giving only his good points.

Apparently their social life had not been extensive, which answered one of the queries that had arisen in Kemp's mind over his client's present extraordinary lack of ready cash. Surely there must be friends to whom she could turn without giving away the facts of her husband's disappearance about which she was understandingly sensitive? But no, no close friends. Acquaintances, she merely said in her soft, rather expressionless voice. Her parents were dead and, despite the boarding-school and tennis parties, left little estate so she had no money of her own. No, there were no relatives to whom she might turn.

If Jessica was to be believed—and in Kemp's mind she was already Jessica and not entirely to be believed since in his experience people rarely told the whole truth in one gulp, which is not the same thing as saying that they invariably lie—Malcolm Moss had been a paragon among husbands. In all their years of marriage no quarrels, no financial anxieties, no women troubles. He gave his wife jewellery on her birthdays, liked to see her well, if conservatively, dressed, stinted nothing on the home or holidays, was kind, attentive, hard-working, entertained sufficiently to keep a small circle of acquaintances but otherwise was not socially inclined. No drinking with the boys, no gambling, no belting round in the ear on Saturday nights, no scenes, tears, fights, recriminations or sulks—in fact none of the usual incidents of marital disharmony which years spent in and around the matrimonial courts, quite apart from his own unhappy personal experience, had convinced Kemp were the norm.

Finally she handed over a photograph. Malcolm Moss looked just as she had described. An ordinary, fair-haired man with a longish face and serious eyes. Kemp felt a fleeting sense of familiarity which he could not place. Perhaps it was simply a too common kind of face.

'Passport?'

'It's still in the bureau at home where he keeps papers. I did look.' She seemed troubled by his inquiry.

'What about cars?'

'That's something else that's odd. Malcolm loved cars. He had a new one every year. I don't drive. That girl must have walked to our door from where she phoned. They left in Malcolm's car but he had told me only the night before that he intended taking it into the garage next day for a service check. It's a white Rover—I'm afraid I don't know the number, I can never remember them... But I'm sure he'd already made an appointment with the garage, and he's very particular about that kind of thing—so he didn't plan to leave...' She looked at Kemp with something like hope in her eyes, but he had little consolation for her.

'Someone else seems to have made the plan, Mrs Moss, and he went along with it.'

So there they were back where they had started. Kemp had a dispiriting set of facts before him. A man at a supposedly dangerous age of life and marriage had left his wife and gone off with a young girl. They both said they were in love, a choice had to be made and he had made it. The oldest tale in the world, a tale of little meaning though the words at the time are always strong; the commonest of matrimonial causes, the same dusty answer. Well, Kemp knew the divorce statistics . . .

'I know,' she was saying, 'but everyone is different.' Again she was on a parallel line of thought. 'Mr Fawcett thinks the same thing. He was sure that if I waited Malcolm would come to some financial arrangement for me. It was I who insisted that we try to find Malcolm immediately . . .' Her voice trailed off into slightly amused wonderment. 'I don't believe I have ever insisted on anything in my life before.'

Kemp could well believe it. She was like a blank page. Even he who prided himself on catching and interpreting those nuances as to character and personality which escape like wary smoke signals from the stoniest of ground, could detect no guide as to what lay behind her strangely light-coloured eyes. There was a perceptive mind inside that head so closely cased in its velour helmet, of that he was certain. He was convinced that she had a drawer full of such hats, that she bought them, unthinking, to match her winter coat because women like her were supposed to do just that. But the choosing of such a hat had nothing to do with the other part of her mind which was only now waking and stretching itself after the long winter sleep of half her life.

'You realize,' he said carefully, 'that this girl could well be someone your husband met in connection with his business. If we find out who she is and find her, then we also find him, and that's what you want?'

'That's what I want.'

'Even if he won't come back?'

She looked at Kemp, or rather she looked at his tie as if speculating whether she liked the pattern. It's not true, he reflected, that you can read people's eyes; there's nothing actually there but the cornea, the retina and moving particles of colour. He felt that if Frances Jessica's eyes were indeed the windows to her soul then they were letting in more light than they gave out.

'Even if he won't come back,' she echoed his words exactly. 'But at least I shall know whether he is safe, and that is what matters.'

She got up, drawing on her glove over the bare fingers no longer enriched by the vast emerald.

Kemp said: 'I shall start with Archer & Co. I agree with Fawcett that the most sensible thing would be for you to phone them and say that Malcolm isn't well and might be away for a few days. Then I'll need your cooperation as to why I'm making inquiries at the firm. Are you capable of lying, Mrs Moss?'

She half smiled. 'Most of us are, Mr Kemp. You mustn't think so highly of me. I thought . . . if you agree . . . I would say you were a friend of ours who wanted a house built and you had been recommended. Or perhaps that Malcolm was thinking of taking you into the business—if that does not sound too far-fetched?'

It did but he didn't say so. He would play it the way she wanted. Having some experience of office gossip,

Kemp suspected the firm might already know more than Mrs Moss did about the blonde girl.

'Even if he's setting up with this other woman it won't affect his business—you must know that. Men are doing it all the time.'

Again she shied away from what was obviously a brutal truth she didn't want to face, so Kemp decided to go along with her suggestion that Archer & Co. were to be given the impression that Malcolm Moss was thinking of taking him into the business; that way he would have more opportunity to look at the books to see if there were any financial as well as amorous entanglements.

He was suddenly struck by a thought. 'You haven't any money...' The position seemed quite ridiculous in view of that ring. Did she expect him to pawn it?

But again she was ready for him.

'Thank you, Mr Kemp,' she said quickly, as if he were about to go for his wallet, 'but Mr Fawcett did advance me a little cash until he gets in touch with the bank. For fares and things...' She smiled, showing the kind of small white teeth Kemp associated with china dolls. 'May I telephone my husband's office from here?'

She took out a notebook, looked up a number and Kemp asked Elvira to get it. Whatever else Mrs Moss kept tucked away under that hat, her husband's telephone number wasn't one of them.

He listened without appearing too curious while she spoke to a Mr Byrne. She seemed to have no difficulty in the gentle art of sophistry.

As he showed her out, they passed McCready himself in the corridor. He raised his hat and gave her a searching glance. Which will tell him damn all, thought Kemp. McCready prided himself on instant appraisals and boasted he could sum up a character in five minutes. He was an ex-policeman and had been a competent officer in his time—which was past—and his experience with the criminal class might well give some justification for his boast, but with others he was less than fallible. In fact he was often dead wrong, but as he paid Kemp's salary, albeit grudgingly, the latter felt it unfair to tell him so. Their present relations were fairly equable. He had taken Lennox Kemp on out of a certain compassion at an ambiguous stage in Kemp's career and Kemp should have been, and frequently was, grateful. But gratitude can be a strain, particularly when accompanied by resentment over the said salary, and that was precisely the point Kemp had been considering so glumly before the advent of Frances Jessica Moss.

Back now at his desk, he picked up the envelope containing the emerald and looked at it, but he didn't open it in case the dangerous green fire should put a further strain on his moral resources. He put the envelope in the safe—which was a misnomer but all they had—and dictated a tape of the interview for Elvira.

TWO

THE OFFICES OF Archer & Co. in Islington looked quietly prosperous and the base for an obviously well-conducted business. Mr Lennox Kemp was politely, even warmly received as a friend of Malcolm Moss, which indicated the high regard in which Jessica's husband was held by his staff. If the red carpet was not exactly rolled out, neither did Kemp feel it was liable to be pulled from under his feet.

Mr Byrne, the office manager, remarked that he understood Mr Moss was having a few days off. 'He has looked a bit tired lately,' he observed, 'only last week I advised him he ought to take a holiday.' There appeared to be no suspicion in the office that Malcolm's indisposition was due to anything other than overwork.

Moss's secretary was a competent woman in her fifties who had been with the firm for fifteen years, and the fact that she was still cheerful spoke volumes for the good relations between herself and her employer.

There were three young men in the drawing-office, and a junior copier and tea-maker, an oblong seventeen-year-old, rather blotchy and distressingly clad in a dark granny print. Wherever Malcolm Moss had found his long-haired blonde, it was certainly not in office hours.

Kemp asked Mr Byrne specifically about work-in-progress, as befitted his role of prospective business partner. He explained that of course Kemp would get fuller details of the balance sheets from the firm's accountants but in the meantime he had no hesitation in showing the working ledgers. From a brief glance there was no doubt that Archer & Co. were doing well; their overheads were not great; Malcolm Moss owned the freehold of the Islington premises; their capacity for work was adequate, and profits from recent contracts fulfilled and estimated costs from work in hand appeared substantial. It was practically a one-man business; there were no partners, just salaried staff. Malcolm Moss on the showing of his firm must be considered a reasonably warm man, financially.

Kemp asked what happened at the branch office in Loughton.

'We opened that a few years ago,' said Mr Byrne, 'and it was going very well. There's a good class of suburban development out there which we couldn't handle from here. We've had some excellent contracts out of the boom in private estates round Epping Forest. Can't think why Malcolm sold it.'

Kemp expressed surprise, and Byrne shrugged. 'Oh well, he's the boss. He got a good price for it—over the odds, actually—and I suppose he wanted the money. Still, it's a great pity.'

'Yes, he did mention the deal,' Kemp said vaguely. 'I wasn't sure it had gone through. In fact I'm particularly interested in the out of town development of the firm—have you any records of the kind of building contracts you had? I know Loughton well—an expanding district for your line of work, I should have thought.'

Mr Byrne obliged smartly with some files from the Loughton branch. They covered, as he explained, the designing of fairly expensive houses. As Kemp handed back one of the folders a set of plans slipped out and attached to one corner was a glossy photograph of a large modern house set in lawns at an attractive angle. Leaning on a white paddock fence in the foreground with a pony beside her was a girl with long straight pale hair, and Kemp immediately saw what Mrs Moss had meant about the lager advertisement. As he fumbled the plans back with the other papers Kemp used the few seconds to glance at the name of the client on the back of the file: Leopold Pearson, Green Acres, High Beech, and the date of the completed contract—just over a month ago.

When Kemp returned to the Agency he phoned Clement Fawcett. He was not exactly his favorite lawyer nor did Fawcett seem very enthusiastic to hear from Kemp.

'Mrs Moss?' he said. 'Yes, I did suggest McCready's might give her some help. This was on her own insistence, you understand. I would have preferred her to wait and take the usual channels. Her husband is a very reputable architect. I don't think a fuss should be made at this point in time.' Kemp often wondered why lawyers invariably used three words when one would do, but supposed that when he had been in the law himself he had done the same, unconsciously. Now he listened to the drone of Fawcett's voice: 'I've known and done business with Moss for many years. He's a man of probity, runs a steady business, no debts, no money troubles. Frankly, I don't believe her story. And I think nothing but harm can come from stirring things up. There's his reputation to consider, and the goodwill of his firm. But she insisted on employing someone immediately to find him, and that's why I suggested McCready's Agency.'

There was an element of distaste in his voice. Thank you for the favour, Mr Fawcett, sir, thought Kemp, but only said: 'Why did he sell his branch at Loughton?'

There was a pause. It could have been simply the usual automatic hesitation solicitors employ when considering what should or should not be divulged, especially to low-class inquiry agents, so Kemp waited.

'You mean the office in High Street, Loughton?'

'Yes.'

'How do you know it's been sold?'

'Well, it has. You must have acted for him. Why did he sell it, and recently too? I understood it was doing very well.'

There was another pause.

Then, very cautiously: 'We have never been instructed in the sale of that property by Mr Moss.'

'Then if you weren't, some other solicitor must have been.'

Kemp imagined Clement Fawcett's face, the lips shutting tight as a purse, his usual expression when affronted. For, if Malcolm Moss had sold his branch office—and Kemp had no doubt from the information given by Mr Byrne that he had done so—then he had done the unforgivable; he had switched solicitors. Well, the niceties of legal professional ethics are no longer my concern, thought Kemp cheerfully, so he pressed on.

'I presume you were acting for him when he bought. Was there any charge on the property or did he hold the deeds himself?'

'We did act when he bought. As I recollect, it was freehold and there was no mortgage necessary. It was a very proper expansion of his growing business. And it must now be worth a very great deal of money...'

'He got over one hundred and fifty thousand for it,' put in Kemp quickly. Byrne had mentioned the figure with some awe.

Fawcett's silence was explicit of his outraged feelings. At length he said: 'This is surprising news to me. Mr Moss mentioned nothing about selling that property and I've spoken to him several times in recent months on other matters...I find this all very hard to believe.'

'Ah well,' said Kemp consolingly, 'even the best clients don't tell their solicitors everything. But don't you think it should be looked into? You could make some discreet inquiries, couldn't you? After all, you're acting for Mrs Moss and you're supposed to be advising her. There's a lot of money floating around somewhere, and she hasn't got any...'

Kemp left the lawyer with that to chew on, knowing that he would soon ferret out which of his professional colleagues had filched a client from him—if the exercise served only to re-establish his own considerable amour-propre.

Although the afternoon was closing in there was still time for a quick run out to Loughton, and indeed when Kemp's car turned into the High Street and found the corner premises which had until so recently been Archer & Co.'s branch office the lights were still on. Byrne had told him that the sale had been to an estate agent anxious to expand from the West End, and Kemp noted that both modernization and uplift had already been applied.

A receptionist sat at a vast glass and chrome desk beneath subdued strip-lighting beside a rubber-plant so new that it had not quite decided whether it would stay where its feet were set in a small square of dry pebbles. The receptionist was the real thing, very cool and classy, and Elvira would have envied her slick black suit. Kemp wondered if she could type. He spun her a fairly coherent story about wanting to buy new property in the area, he had been recommended to

Archer & Co. by a very satisfied client of Mr Malcolm Moss, the architect—a Mr Pearson who had had a house Green Acres at High Beech designed for him—could she perhaps tell him where he could contact Mr Moss? When he stopped for breath and smiled idiotically at the young lady as if there and then she could deliver him up Mr Moss out of the hollow of her hands, she got a word in.

She explained that the offices no longer belonged to Archer & Co., that Mr Moss would probably still be available at Islington, but that of course they being Benson & Partners from Kensington would be happy to supply his needs—Mr er ... ?

'Mr Lennox,' said Kemp, 'I've only seen a photograph of this Green Acres house but it looked just the kind of thing I'm after. Perhaps I'll go and have a look at it, and see if there are any sites nearby on which I could build.'

Having established himself as a prospective purchaser, Kemp had no difficulty in continuing their chat well beyond the six o'clock close-down, as the young lady hastened to assure him that her position was more elevated than mere receptionist—she was a negotiator and anxious to demonstrate both her charm and salesmanship. Not only did she tell him where Green Acres was—although she knew nothing of the new owner—and show him estate plans of other properties being built in the district, but she also gave him information about her employers' purchase of the offices from Archer & Co. Benson & Partners had been pleasantly surprised to find it on the market, and had been prepared to pay a good price for the property and goodwill. Apparently the essential factor had been speed so far as Mr Moss had been concerned. And secrecy, thought Kemp, remembering Fawcett. In his role as a complete stranger to the area he put in a casual query about local solicitors and was told by the knowledgeable young woman that in fact Benson & Partners had used their own London legal associates for the purchase, and Mr Moss had agreed they should also act for him in his sale. Repressing a shudder of horror at this breach of professional etiquette, Kemp reflected that Moss must have been in one hell of a hurry to get the deal through—presumably he needed the money as part of his plans for himself and the long-haired blonde. Beautiful young girls like that don't come cheap.

Gathering up his wad of sales literature and thanking the eager receptionist who would obviously go far if she kept this up, Kemp went out into the twilight.

At the top of the High Street a side road slid away sharply into the gloom of the Forest. He hesitated for a moment. He had no valid reason to call on Mr Pearson but his curiosity was roused, he might as well take a look at the place. He turned his car from the lights of Loughton and accelerated up the dark hill towards High Beech.

THREE

THE FOREST AT DUSK closes its ranks against visitors. In the daytime when picnickers spill out of their cars and set up temporary homes with folding chairs and sandwiches the trees stay aloof and indifferent; such small trite domesticities are not for them. But when night falls the gnarled trunks get together, leaning on each other like old men while their leaves gossip, snigger and threaten.

Or so it seemed to Lennox Kemp as he drove through their shadows. The thought lasted just long enough to be dismissed as mere capitulation to Ruskin's 'pathetic fallacy'—personal feelings engendering in external surroundings an impression that nature must be at one with the beholder. If his mood was bleak, then any hostility in the trees must simply be an emanation of his own mood bounced back. For in actual fact the Forest was just a place where trees were still permitted to live, beginning on this particular road with the suddenness which translates planning theory into practical terms, theoretical lines on development maps binding the factual existence of a green belt. The place had been tamed, it should hold no terrors now.

Neither did Kemp consider himself to be a stranger to the Forest; he knew its ways, its paths, like the veins on the backs of his hands. At one time he had regarded it as an extension of his own garden. He had walked his dogs there, kicked through the autumn leaves while rehearsing speeches for next day's court appearances, done his mental homework while he trampled the sparse undergrowth, the unseen mosses, the dead wood of stricken branches, never marking their fall nor in spring noticing the first green curl of bracken or the pale desperate stance of early saplings. But these days were gone; perhaps the Forest was now taking its revenge for his insouciance.

He stopped his car in a gladeway and walked softly over the turf made spongy from recent rain towards the white paddock fence glimmering faintly through the underbrush. The trees had drawn the dusk round them like a shawl and the air was still.

There was a wide gateway and the name Green Acres. Kemp walked along the outside fence, looking in. The house lay behind wide lawns. It had been built ranch-style and there was an atmosphere of well-spent money about its secluded privacy. He reflected that there must have been deft handling of the planning angle; money does not necessarily corrupt the authorities—even his cynicism did not go that far—but it can help to smooth the path of private aspiration in that as in other fields.

The hornbeams seemed to agree with him, raising their short tough limbs in horror, or perhaps they were simply hanging about for some unplanned cataclysm,

or queuing up for some arboreal party to which man
would not be invited.

Kemp stopped and listened to the whisper of their
leaves and heard, far below, the faint roar of traffic on
the coloured roads into the Metropolis. Here London
seemed far away, yet near enough for this Forest to
have been its playground. Children had trailed wilted
bluebells back from here to jars on Stepney window-
sills; youths had cycled out on dusty Sunday after-
noons to be photographed in solemn sepia groups
outside the vast Victorian pub on the height. There
had been even then a darker side; fleeing rogues found
a refuge here, robbers hid their spoils, and beneath the
ferny floor still lay the pathetic bones of London's
unwanted babies. Well, it belonged to them—the
common people of London, given to them as Caesar
gave to the commoners of Rome his private arbours
this side Tiber, to recreate themselves. The Royals who
had planned it, hunted it, and finally given it away had
had no further use for it—the gift had been no great
sacrifice.

Kemp cursed the Forest for the effect it was having
on him. He began to feel that he had no real purpose
here, he had nothing definite to investigate and no
positive reason to call on Mr Leopold Pearson, the
owner of Green Acres.

Nevertheless he went back to the gateway, put a
tentative finger on the centre post and it swung open
silently on a well-oiled hinge. He slipped through the
gate and walked quickly up the side of the lawn. There

was a car in the driveway at the side of the house and although it was in shadow it seemed to be a white car, and a large one. He simply had to get a closer look at it.

Afterwards he was to argue with himself that it was the dark influence of the Forest which made him act in the way he did—a way which was to have repercussions on many people beside himself, for in such split seconds of time are sown the dragon teeth of future events. But, even as he trod the short grass of the lawn rather than risk making a noise on the gravel, he felt he was unprepared, he had let his mind wander in self-indulgent introspection instead of formulating a sensible and proper method of intruding upon the privacy of Green Acres.

He was half way across the garden when the porch light was suddenly switched on sending out a brilliant glare over the driveway and catching him within its beam. Without a second's thought he leapt into the nearest flowerbed, and lay there motionless, the heavy scent of wallflowers in his nostrils. He heard voices and through a screen of stems and leaves saw two men emerge on to the porch. Their voices were raised as if in argument but Kemp was too far away to make out their words.

One man opened the door, got in and started the engine. Then the other man ran forward shouting;

'You damn fool, the boot's still open!'

The car engine continued to run but the driver got out and walked round to the back. But then he was facing Kemp's hiding-place so Kemp ducked his head down and lay flat. He heard the noise of a boot lid being raised, the crunch of feet on gravel, then silence. It lasted too long for his curiosity so he lifted his head cautiously and looked out.

Both men had their backs to him as they leaned in over the opened boot. They seemed to be pulling at some long heavy weight. A roll of carpet, a bag of golf clubs? Whatever it was, there was considerable difficulty in stowing what seemed an intransigent cargo, all the time conducting a muttered colloquy just beyond the range of Kemp's ears.

Somewhere on the far side of the house a dog barked. Kemp brought his head down smartly and tried to become one with his leafy surroundings. If a dog came bounding across the lawn the game was up. Desperately he clutched at plausible excuses for being so found, ignominiously hiding on enclosed premises after dark, but for all his normal inventiveness he could no more conjure up a likely story than he could move his limbs from their earthy bed. He had created the situation; he was stuck with it.

In the space of time it took to frame even such incoherent thoughts events outran them. He heard the slam of the boot lid, the scrape of hurried feet on gravel, the closing of both car doors. There was a screech of ill-used tyres as the vehicle was wrenched round in a circle and driven off down the drive, passing a few yards from his hideout. He raised his head as he heard it slow at the gate which had swung shut, and he watched as the man on the passenger side jumped out and opened it. The car barely paused for him to get in again, then it was off at high speed.

Only then did Kemp run to where he had left his own car, listening for the sound of their engine to determine the direction taken. They seemed to be climbing further up into the denser part of the Forest as he slipped the Morris out on to the upward road in pursuit.

Yet he lost them. When he stopped at the crossroads where the lanes diverge towards the little church, the Royal Oak and the wide expanse of picnic ground, he could hear nothing. He knew they must be somewhere in those narrow roads. If their car had been driven towards the main highway then he should still have heard it. There was no sound except the night wind stirring the branches and the muted echo of faraway traffic below the Forest.

Kemp lit a cigarette, wrote the car number on the packet, and gazed out at the hornbeams. They didn't look very friendly, but then it was no concern of theirs that the car had been a white Rover and presumably one of the occupants the runaway husband. Unless... But conjecture at this stage could only breed meaningless fancies. The practical question for Kemp was should he report to his client, and what?

He drove home to his nondescript three-room flat in Walthamstow in a mood of disgruntled self-criticism. He knew he had bungled it. That stupid leap into the obscurity of a flowerbed had been, at the very least, inept, precluding a proper approach both to the owner of Green Acres and the owner of the white car. What disturbed Kemp more was that the answer lay in his own psyche as to why he had thrown himself so unhesitatingly into hiding. The Forest and its power over him had stirred too many memories, drawn too near the bone of old forgotten battles he preferred to leave alone. He had allowed himself the dangerous luxury of a moment's personal weakness, lost his concentration on the job in hand, and in doing so he had botched a perfectly feasible line of inquiry.

It was with reluctance, and only out of a sense of duty, that he dialled the Crownberry Avenue number and heard it ring. He let it go on ringing even as he placed the receiver on the table in front of him and looked at it. He rang again later—it was nearly midnight—but there was still no reply.

Well, well, so there was no anxious wife sitting by the phone awaiting news of her missing husband. Kemp went to bed but his sleep was disturbed by dreams in which he was trying to shake the truth out of a woman with curiously light brown eyes under an absurd hat.

FOUR

ELVIRA, QUITE REASONABLY, objected to working on Saturdays. She deemed McCready's to be a professional office—although heaven knows from what sociological angle she took her criteria—and she said only tradespeople opened their doors on a Saturday. Elvira had an unerring instinct for trends and was justifiably smug when the banks upheld her view.

When there was any work for them the operatives did foregather for the minimum time prior to adjournment to the pub, but there was little doing at the moment, so that Kemp found himself alone and making a solitary cup of coffee when the phone rang at ten-thirty. He had hoped to hearten himself in this way before reporting last night's fiasco to his client.

He knew her soft voice immediately. It seemed merely an extension of a dream, for he had slept badly and Frances Jessica had wandered in and out among other images.

'Mr Kemp?'

'Yes. Kemp speaking. That's Mrs Moss, isn't it?'

'I'm so glad you're there. I have some wonderful news. I have to tell you that the wanderer has returned.'

Kemp didn't say anything. Her voice was light and cheerful. Not at all like the voice that he had heard in his dreams.

'Yes, Malcolm has come back. He came in this morning. Well, just over an hour ago. Everything is going to be all right. It's all over. I mean that business of the girl. Are you there, Mr Kemp?'

Kemp felt a sudden surge of anger, an anger he couldn't understand. He wanted to swear, kick the desk, throw the telephone across the room. So he was rough.

'You'll want your emerald back? It's quite safe, Mrs Moss. Do you want to send for it? I don't suppose you want me to bring it—in the circumstances with your husband there that wouldn't do, I'm sure...'

He had forgotten how quickly she could match his tone. 'Of course it's all right,' she said briskly. 'I've told him all about it. We both wondered whether—' There was a pause which Kemp made no attempt to bridge—'you would bring it back yourself. You were so kind yesterday. Would you visit us and bring it? It would be...more friendly. And of course we want to pay you for your time.'

Kemp choked back a retort which might have served to appease his wounded feelings, and said politely:

'Yes, if you wish me to. Whenever you like.'

'Perhaps this evening? You have our address. I should like to say come and have dinner with us but Malcolm is still not at all well. He doesn't feel up to seeing anyone. But could you come and have a drink with us, say about seven?'

It was all too dreadfully banal. An invitation to cocktails; a successful architect and his lady wife asking a somewhat dubious inquiry agent to have a drink with them—but not of course to dinner. Kemp realized wearily that he was just being stupid. All right, perhaps these people had been having him on—and he had justification for being angry—but this was no time for class-conscious nitpicking.

'Yes, I'll come—and I'll certainly bring your ring.'

He sat back and drank his cold coffee. He looked out of the dusty window and told himself firmly to put the whole matter into perspective; this had just been another case, closed almost before it opened. And, as in such cases, he would be paid. Out of what, then, was coming this bitterness? The sooner he got Frances Jessica out of his hair, the better. Gradually, sane thought took over—and the instinctive curiosity which made him a better detective than he had been lawyer. Yes, he wanted very much to know the end of the story, and he certainly wanted to meet, and judge for himself, this paragon of husbands, the sinner who had erred and strayed like a lost sheep but was now, it seemed, returned and welcomed back within the fold.

Kemp took the envelope from the safe and opened it. The ring rolled comfortably out into his hand, and he put it in his pocket and went downstairs.

Joseph Crohn kept a small shop down a side street near the market. In days past pawnbroking had been a necessary adjunct to such an area but with rising affluence that part of the business had declined and the little dusty window reflected the trend towards antiques with trays of Victorian jet pieces, corals and dubious amber necklaces, jumbled together with tarnished silver, and chipped china miniature chamber pots picturing Southend pier. Crohn was an astute man; he knew that, given the vagaries of fashion, some day there would be collectors even of such oddities.

He was also a good jeweller and kept his nose clean as far as the police were concerned. He gave Kemp as sharp a look as his half-glasses permitted, and disappeared into the back workshop with the ring. When he came back he grunted:

'It's not stolen, if that's all you wanted to know,' he said, 'Leastways, not on any lists I've got. Don't suppose it's yours, eh, Kemp? Agency business?'

Kemp nodded. 'Belongs to a client. What do you think of it?'

Crohn held it up to the light.

'That's a very valuable emerald. Of course the setting's not worthy of it. Good enough, twenty-two carat gold, but a stone like that deserves something better—it's a beauty. Fetch a big price. Your client thinking of selling?'

Kemp took the ring back. He shook his head.

'I don't think so. Thanks, Joe.'

Kemp drove out to Crownberry Avenue that evening in a mood of some disenchantment with life. He had the uneasy feeling of being just on the edge of something he didn't understand, and that in some way he had been used, but the suspicion was so nebulous that contemplation of it only increased his sense of frustration.

No. 72 was at the higher end of the road—the end that had not yet deteriorated. There was a low stone wall, a pillared gateway, laurels on either side, and a modest drive leading to a double-fronted stone house probably built in the spacious days before the First World War; not a large house but solid, and unobtrusively and decently modernized.

Mrs Moss came to the door herself.

This time Lennox Kemp took a closer look at her. She had for some twenty-four hours taken over his thoughts, shaken him out of a delusion of complacency, caught him as it were on the hop. He resented the effect she had had on him, and his reaction was to hope that she was flawed. So as he followed her into the hall—which was just a hall, no marble columns— Kemp glanced at her legs. He had the sudden savage wish that she should have, if not feet of clay, at least thick ankles. She wore a brown silky dress with a small pattern, a dress neither mini nor maxi, neither chic nor dowdy, and her stockings were serviceable denier rather than sheer, but alas for his hostile hope, her ankles were impeccable.

Trying to come to terms with his feelings of illogical animosity, he was momentarily deprived of his usual powers of observance so that it was not until he had crossed the threshold and shaken hands with the man who half-rose from the sofa that Kemp realized that the room was not only pleasant but beautiful. The proportions incidental to similar houses of its period had been unaffected by such subtle modernization as had taken place. The ornate stucco clusters where flowers and eggs were inextricably intertwined in the dim corners of the high ceiling must have been there when the house was built, but the pale Adam green walls and the dusky rose furnishings were in the light modern manner rather than examples of Edwardian exuberance.

Malcolm Moss was certainly the man in the photograph which Kemp had seen but now he looked ill. His skin was unhealthy and his eyelids shadowed as they drooped over eyes which avoided his visitor's. It was understandable. He could hardly have wanted to meet Kemp.

He apologized for not feeling well, and sank back on to the sofa as Kemp sat down opposite while Frances Jessica handed drinks. When they were settled Kemp took out the envelope which he had resealed and gave it to her.

'Your ring is in there, Mrs Moss, and also the paper you signed.'

She took it and went and sat on the arm of the sofa beside her husband. She made no attempt to open the envelope.

'We're both most grateful to you, Mr Kemp,' she said in her soft, even voice. 'And of course we'll pay your expenses and your fee.'

'I'm afraid you must think we've wasted a good deal of your time,' Malcolm Moss said heavily. 'I'm sorry, but I can't really explain exactly what happened. It's something now only between my wife and myself...'

Kemp waited, sipping his sherry, which was good but unexceptionally so. Mrs Moss took her husband's hand and he turned towards her. When they were gazing into each other's eyes Kemp began to feel like an intruder.

'There's no need to explain, Mr Moss. I'm glad for your wife's sake that things worked out all right, but that is, as you say, between yourselves. So far as the Agency is concerned we shall simply close our file, and that's an end to it.'

'I told you, Malcolm, that Mr Kemp is a very understanding kind of man.' Mrs Moss smiled at Kemp and went on with all the earnest sincerity of a heroine in a bad movie, 'You must think us both very foolish people to have involved you in our small domestic upset. You have been most kind.'

Malcolm Moss became practical. He asked for particulars of Kemp's fee and expenses, and Kemp said make the cheque payable to the Agency; he couldn't help thinking about young Albert who was eaten by the lion—How much to settle this matter? Well, how much do you usually pay? For, to Kemp, the situation had begun to have the same element of farce and, after he had downed two sherries and they had sat and talked about the weather and the state of the country, the feeling grew until he feared he might become hysterical. Since he had known himself in that state before and might not be answerable for his behaviour, he made his excuses and left.

He did not drive straight home. He went to the nearest spot where he could safely park his car, and chain-smoked desperately for an hour.

Something was wrong. He knew it in his bones. But whether it was with the Mosses or with himself he could not be sure. He seemed to have lost his faculty for objective thinking. He felt hollow, yet furiously angry. Had he indeed been taken for a ride? And if so, why? Slowly he dismissed the idea; Frances Jessica Moss had been sincere enough when she came to the Agency, unless she was a good actress. As to Malcolm Moss himself, there was no doubt the man was ill. But equally any man who had left his wife in the circumstances she had put to Kemp, and then returned six days later, would at the very least appear upset and anxious. She must have been satisfied with whatever explanation he had offered. By now she must know much more than Kemp did. Except perhaps for the one vital fact of which Kemp himself was certain; as he had turned his car into the drive of 72 Crownberry Avenue the garage doors had been open, and inside was the white Rover. Kemp had had no need to refer to his cigarette packet; he had remembered the number anyway.

FIVE

LENNOX KEMP PUSHED the thin file of the Moss papers to the back of the Accounts Paid cabinet and tried to consider the matter closed, despite nagging doubt like intermittent toothache that it ought to go under Unfinished Business.

He had long given up the youthful hope that there is in life some earthly paradise just around the next bend, or that through some small doorway there is a rose-garden if only one could shrink oneself in size and get into it. It was not entirely that he lived from day to day in quiet desperation, simply that he had made up his mind that life on the whole didn't make much sense, that it alternated between high tragedy and hilarious farce and the longer the dull intermissions between, the better for his sanity. He had no desire to be once more pulled about by forces stronger than himself, and had decided to follow the old cure for melancholia such as his—don't look too far ahead, indeed no further than tea-time.

Just before the Summer recess he had been up at the Law Courts on a couple of divorces and took the tube back home. He bought an evening paper and glanced through the news as the carriage rattled and swayed. He looked at the cricket scores, and the foreign news, as usual full of menace and foreboding. There was scandal on every page; even the business section featured a petulant boardroom walk-out. Must be the heat, he thought, and realized he was depressed. There had been too many sleazy divorces, too many sly watchings and waitings, too many times serving too many writs; too many frightened people. He decided it was time he took a holiday. He folded the paper, and a small item caught his eye:

EPPING FOREST BODY; WOMAN IDENTIFIED.

Kemp read on:

'At the inquest today in Epping Court the brother of the woman whose body was found last week in the Wake Pond gave evidence as to her identity.'

A name leapt from the page, and Kemp read the whole paragraph through carefully. It said that a Mr Leopold Pearson of Green Acres, High Beech, had given evidence that his sister Lucille Pearson had left their home in May saying that she was returning to America. They had planned such a trip together but he had been detained in England on business and she had booked her flight to go alone. Replying to the Coroner's questions, Mr Pearson disclosed that his sister had been ill and depressed for some years, that she had decided she would be happier in the States where they had formerly lived, and her brother had no reason to suppose that she had not gone. In answer to a further question Mr Pearson said it was not unusual that his sister had not written to him; she was in the habit of travelling about on her own, and he had understood she was to join friends in America. He did not know them and it had never occurred to him that she had not joined them. He had been shocked and distressed when the police contacted him with evidence that the woman's body found in the pond might be that of his sister. Evidence was given that a handbag found in the pond near the body belonged to Miss Pearson. A local doctor in Leatown gave evidence that Miss Pearson had been his patient, that she was mentally unstable and suffered from acute depression. It was found that Miss Pearson had taken her life while the balance of her mind was disturbed, and the Coroner expressed sympathy for the bereaved brother.

Kemp tucked the paper under his arm and went home to steady his mind, and curb speculations which were off in all directions like runaway horses.

What business was it of his, he argued later, sitting with late coffee in his nondescript flat turning out his mental pockets rationally to see exactly what he had in them? A name, a place, a time of year, a disappearance and a death—these constituted one set of facts. Another comprised a second disappearance, a photograph, the same place and one man's car. Coincidence? He didn't trust coincidences, they smacked too much of gods above pulling strings.

Yet why should he interfere? No one was going to pay him for it. Even if, as he suspected, Malcolm Moss was concerned in the death of Lucille Pearson, why should he, Kemp, play the instrument of justice? Yet, even as he sorted through the odd pieces of information knocking about in his head, he was conscious that his depression was lifting, the mood of lethargy and ennui evaporating, and he knew he could not resist the joys of the chase, the urge to investigate, his own inherent curiosity.

The motivation for most decisions has bastard qualities; he was bored with his job, he was lonely (the undertow played on that weak edge), he had money in his pocket and McCready owed him a two-week holiday. It wasn't sharp enough to be called determination, he simply felt himself drifting with a current which happened to be flowing in one direction. He did not particularly cherish the notion that there is anything as heavy as a destiny that shapes our ends but acknowledged that there are moments of vacancy in life when outside forces are allowed to enter—and this seemed just such a moment for him. The man who caught Death's eye in Baghdad and prudently removed to Samarkand did not escape; Death looked down his list and said: 'Strange, I have that fellow down—for Samarkand . . .'

So it was that Kemp a few days later took a busman's holiday, and headed for Leatown.

SIX

LEATOWN LIES ON the opposite side of the Forest to
Loughton, and far from being merely a suburb of
London, it is a market town of some antiquity and interest. Although the inquest on Lucille Pearson had
been held at Epping, the local police station was in
Leatown and so was the doctor who had given evidence, so it seemed to Kemp the logical place to be-
gin.

As he drove out to it through the teeming streets and
traffic of Tottenham and Edmonton he realized his
own knowledge of the place would be both hindrance
and help. Before his personal little world had fallen
apart he had lived there, enjoyed a wide circle of
friends, professional and social, owned a house there
which he had now for years avoided as he had all his
former associates. He might well find himself heading towards trouble again, stumble once more into that
morass of unspoken condemnation, the embarrassed
conversations that skirted dangerous topics, the
glances that slid away, the assumed heartiness that es-
chewed proper judgement. But, he told himself as he
neared the town, all that was over six years ago, it
would be long forgotten—at least he hoped so.

The town had changed little. The High Street had been given a lick of fresh paint. The attractive plaster façades above the shops had received a coat or two of not unpleasing pale tangerine, sugar pink or cream, the whole effect negated at one end of the street by the demolition of what he remembered as a black-and-white pub, not perhaps an authentic piece but it had had a certain cockeyed charm; in its place was a brick-built monstrosity labelled the Leatown Community Centre. He wished it luck but without much enthusiasm. No communal activity had ever succeeded in Leatown; an early Essex country strain was still strong in the inhabitants, who kept to themselves in the full meaning of the phrase—which was often on their lips and expressed with pride and conviction. They didn't hold with getting together on anything, as various culture-loving bodies had learned to their cost.

Kemp drove into the car park behind the Town Hall and found a space in a corner where willowherb grew boldly out of the stone wall. The car park was warm, enclosed and quiet as a cloister. Kemp sat for a while and pondered on what sources he could tap. There were several and he felt no enthusiasm for any of them, but even if it meant stirring up old trouble for himself he knew that if he didn't make a start on his inquiries the buzz of unanswered doubts would continue to affect his mind like a swarm of bees looking for somewhere to settle.

As he walked up the High Street he felt he was playing a part, and the role was not unattractive—

Ishmael, the Outsider, the Return of the Native—but Kemp knew he could not measure up to it. Although tragedy had once overtaken him he could never achieve the tragic look; he might feel as sardonic as Bogart but he still looked like an amiable teddybear. Sorrow had not etched fine lines on his bumpy forehead nor given his pale eyes the hint of sadness proper to his situation. If indeed he had become a part of all that he had known, it simply didn't show.

Where should he go first? Tinker, tailor, soldier, sailor, lawyer, doctor, police? The doctor's gate came nearest so he turned in there.

The plate at the door above the little box where prescriptions were neatly held down by pebbles told him that of the original partnership of three one had gone and was replaced by a new name, Dr Benjamin Seft—the name in the newspaper account, Lucille Pearson's doctor. Dr Robin Plender's name was still on the plate. Kemp and his former wife Muriel had been on dining terms with Robin and Betty Plender. Kemp had no wish to trade on that old friendship now but it might at least get his foot in the door.

It was a stranger who answered his ring. A tall untidy man of middle years with reddish hair and very round blue eyes that had the lustre of enamel beads.

'Is Dr Plender in? I'm an old friend of his and I was passing through Leatown and thought I would look him up.'

'No. He's out on his rounds. Sorry.'

He didn't appear very forthcoming but doctors at that time of day tend to be busy people.

'Well, I wonder if you perhaps can help me. I think you may be Dr Seft? This wouldn't take up much of your time.'

'Yes, I am Dr Seft. You might as well come in.' He stood to one side and let Kemp pass. He opened the inner door leading to the surgery. The place hadn't changed much. The filing boxes were as battered as ever, the big desk still held too many papers and objects. Robin Plender had never been very tidy, and used to admit that new systems baffled him.

Dr Seft sat down behind the desk and Kemp took the other chair, wondering if the interview might be easier if he simply asked for a prescription for chilblains.

'What can I do for you?' The doctor's manner was not ungracious in the circumstances.

'I know Dr Plender was the police surgeon here some years ago...' Kemp began.

'I've taken over these duties.'

'Ah well, you can probably tell me what I want to know. This is my line of business, by the way.' He flipped him over one of the Agency cards. He was quite accustomed to seeing faces harden and shutters come down over eyes at the sight of the piece of pasteboard so he wasn't altogether surprised at getting such a reaction now.

Dr Seft fingered the card distastefully.

'You say you're an old friend of Dr Plender's? Perhaps you'd better see him. What case is it you're interested in?'

'That inquest the other day in Epping. The woman's body that was found in the Forest. I wondered if you could give me some information about her.'

Dr Seft continued to look at Kemp's card as though the writing on it was as obscure as that on the Rosetta stone.

Eventually after a long pause he spoke, choosing his words with care.

'You mean of course, Miss Pearson? I'm afraid I must ask you first what has prompted your inquiries?'

'It happens that I have a client,' said Kemp, seeking shelter in the circumlocutory language one employs when mixing an element of truth with airy fiction, 'who read of the death and wondered if she might have known the deceased...' There was a splinter of fact there; after all, Jessica Moss had met Lucille Pearson once—of that Kemp was certain.

'May I ask the name of your client?' Dr Seft was polite enough but Kemp sensed it was mere superficial courtesy and nothing else.

'I'm afraid I can't tell you that. Only that my client was upset by the news of Miss Pearson's death and asked me to inquire into the circumstances surrounding it.'

Dr Seft let the card drop from his fingers as if it were a particularly harmful bacteria. 'You realize you are treading in a very delicate area, Mr—er—Kemp. I hope you do not intend to bother Miss Pearson's brother with these inquiries. He has had a very distressing experience...'

'I was hoping that you, as her doctor, might be able to give me more details of the unhappy young lady. Of course I would not dream of intruding on a brother's natural grief it it could be avoided...'

Dr Benjamin Seft had extraordinary bright eyes. Behind them Kemp felt there was a keen intelligence. At the moment they were speculative as though the doctor was assessing his visitor, summing him up and adding him to some store of statistical information. Perhaps it was the normal reaction of a keen medical man to a new patient; Kemp began to wonder if the tone of his skin or the bumps on his forehead held symptoms of incipient malady.

'I should not recommend you to visit Mr Leopold Pearson,' Dr Seft was saying smoothly, 'at this time. Perhaps later—when he has recovered... There must be other channels that you can dredge in your—er—line of work. And I'm quite certain that I cannot help you. It would be quite unethical of me to discuss a patient with you...'

'Even when she's dead?' Kemp was brusque; medical ethics, like legal ethics, could be used as a cloak to cover up iniquities just as often as they were used as a defence of confidences.

The doctor was on his feet, and with a sudden movement was at the door and holding it open. Kemp had no option but to go through it.

'I'm sorry you feel like that, Dr Seft. I was only making perfectly reasonable inquiries . . .'

'Then I suggest you take your inquiries elsewhere.'

Benjamin Seft was a swift mover; already he was at the front door and practically propelling Kemp out and down the step.

'There are proper channels for that sort of thing. Good morning, Mr Kemp.'

Mr Kemp was left unceremoniously on the doorstep gazing at the brass knocker in the shape of an angry lion as the door was slammed in his face. Well, well, he thought, what an exceedingly touchy fellow. A difficult surgery, a hangover, a chip on his shoulder, or a perfectly correct professional attitude towards inquiry agents—probably classed way down among the hypnotists and faith-healers?

Somewhat shaken by the encounter, Kemp decided to test his reception at the police station, but he needn't have worried; the desk sergeant was new and had obviously never heard of Lennox Kemp when he presented his card. The first one, he now realized, still lay on the desk at the inhospitable surgery.

Kemp again spun the tale about the lady who had engaged him: she had met a Miss Pearson and lost touch with her, she wondered whether it could be the same person. The sergeant was very helpful and let him see their reports. After all, the inquest was over, no further action was being taken. Kemp glanced rapidly through the papers he produced. Leopold Pearson had been able to furnish the police with a photograph which was still attached to the file.

Kemp saw once more the resemblance to his girl of the poster, the cool, slightly insolent look in the eyes, the long face sliced down either side by the fall of straight blonde hair.

He memorized as much as he needed, and returned to the quiet of the car park at midday to scribble notes.

Everything seemed to support the verdict reached. Lucille Pearson had been a fairly neurotic young lady, she had suffered from intermittent periods of deep depression, and there was a record of more than one suicide attempt while under psychiatric treatment in America. Both she and her brother were citizens of the United States but he had business connections in London, and they had settled in the new house in the Forest to give him access to these interests, and at the same time to give his sister quiet surroundings in which it was hoped she might recover. But it had not worked out; Lucille Pearson had made few friends in the district, he himself was busy, so she had finally decided to return to the States. All her luggage had been forwarded in advance and had in fact arrived at the apartment she still kept in New York so that when she left Green Acres she was only carrying a shoulder-bag, the remnants of which had been found deep in the mud of the Wake Pond, but it had been good leather and was identified by both Leopold Pearson and Miss

Pearson's maid. The waterlogged contents revealed what could have been a passport and travel documents. A search at London Airport had disclosed that a flight had been booked by Miss Pearson for May 13 but had not been taken up. Her brother had to attend a business meeting in the Midlands that morning and had left the house at nine o'clock after saying good-bye to his sister. She had told him a taxi was coming to take her to the airport for her afternoon flight but no such taxi had been traced. It was suggested that in fact she had never intended to return to America. Instead, in a fit of depression she had wandered off into the Forest and drowned herself.

Kemp skipped the surmises; much more to the point was the report of the Home Office pathologist: the body had been decomposing, consistent with its having been immersed in water for possibly three months, but the process had been slowed because the natu-rally-rising corpse had been stuck below a rotting jetty and been partially preserved in mud at the bottom of the pond. Enough for identification, wondered Kemp with some scepticism. But there was evidence firmer than human flesh: not only the bag but a gold wrist-watch marked 'Lucille Pearson' had sent the local police straight up to Green Acres.

The police sergeant had been, if anything, disap-pointed that identification had taken place so quickly. For a couple of days they had enjoyed the attentions of the press avid for news of the mystery woman whose body had turned up so tragically in their local pond, but now the case was closed and the interest and drama had faded. The sergeant hinted—like all policemen do in that haunted area—that lots of bodies still lay 'neath the Forest's ferny floor, although he didn't quite put it like that. London's playground, thought Kemp, and London's burial ground for centuries for those who disappeared and about whom there were to be no questions asked...

Well, he was asking the questions now.

He noted the dates, sat back and looked at them. She was to have flown to America on Saturday, May 13—obviously flying in the face of superstition. Good brother Leo had had pressing business elsewhere, and said he did not return to Green Acres until the following week, and assumed his little sister was safely in the States.

And this girl—for Kemp was certain now that it could be no other—had come to Crownberry Avenue on Sunday, May 7, and cheekily appropriated Malcolm Moss from under the eyes of his wife. On Friday night, May 12, Lennox Kemp, submerged in flowers, had watched two men struggling with a burden in the boot of Moss's car.

It didn't take a genius to work it out: the burden had been the body of Lucille Pearson. Any heavy-footed detective could have reached that conclusion without damaging his cerebellum. The question Kemp had to answer was: what was he going to do about it?

Before going to see—despite the admonition of Dr Seft—Leopold Pearson, the so-caring brother who

seemed to have made such a good impression on the
police and the Coroner, Kemp decided that the latter
must be his next port of call.

The coroner, old Trumball.

But he had to go into the pub in the middle of the
High Street and sit for half an hour over a strong
whisky before he plucked up enough courage for the
call. Despite what he hoped was a hard carapace of
indifference self-imposed during the last six years, it
took an effort of will to push open the familiar reeded
glass door that announced Trumball, Egerton & Har-
ris, Solicitors, in gold letters. When that gold letter-
ing had first been put up it had read Trumball,
Egerton & Kemp. Well, no use thinking of that now;
if all the water under all the bridges flowed backwards it still couldn't change things.

There was an adenoidal girl in reception, she didn't
know him, which was a relief.

'I'm sorry. Mr Trumball has gone for lunch.'

As she spoke the inner door opened and a man came
through with a bundle of documents. He glanced at
Kemp, then stared. He coloured slightly, and there
seemed to Kemp an interminable period of hesitation
before Tony Egerton came over to him with out-
stretched hand.

'Why, Lennox . . . It's good to see you.'

'Hullo, Tony. How are you?'

Egerton, the middle partner, the buffer, but a good
man nevertheless; he had been fair to Kemp, and now
it was he who regained his composure first.

'Come on in,' he said, leading Kemp through to his room overlooking the High Street. In a sudden flash of realization Lennox Kemp saw that his own deliberate isolation during the last few years might have bred in him a sort of conceit. Tony Egerton had probably not given him a thought, censorious or otherwise, over these years. And as they talked he felt his tension lessen, and he began to apprehend that he might have been wrong to avoid his former colleagues. What was still to him in the worst of times an unhealed wound, at the best a familiar toothache, to them was past history. Life, and business, went on. Crises were met each day, pressures rose and fell, problems were shaken out, reduced to basics, solved or simply shelved to gather dust in files forgotten; counsels' opinions urgently debated at the time now mouldered finally within their faded pink tapes, the contentious emotions they once engendered at last cooled and dead. The atmosphere in this familiar office which he had once inhabited was soothing, and he felt his mind clearing and some of the old professional sharpness returning.

Tony Egerton was an amusing talker, and had a wit at variance with his bland pink forehead and short-sighted grey eyes, for his tongue could be scathing or even downright wicked. Clients thought him an old pet but he was as ruthless as an alligator when he liked.

It was a happy accident that Kemp should meet him now. Although old Trumball was the coroner, Tony did much of the legwork. Someone had to do it to allow the old man the time to burrow into byeways of esoteric knowledge and produce the plums which occasionally astounded and impressed his Coroner's Court.

Tony knew all about the Pearson case, and had no doubt about the verdict being correct.

'What sort of man is the brother?' Kemp asked.

'Very reasonable. Company director. Import and export business—in a pretty big way. In and out of America and Europe—you know the kind of thing. Seemed a decent sort. Very cut up about his sister but all the evidence showed she'd been a thorough neurotic. Plenty of money about both of them, incidentally. I hear he's selling up the house and going back to the States. Can't blame him—very distressing...'

'Had you done any business for them?'

'No. They weren't local people in any way. They'd spent most of their life abroad until his business interests brought him to London, and they had this house built for them at High Beech. Quite a place, I gather. The plot alone must have cost them a packet.'

'You didn't know who built their house, or who designed it?'

Tony shook his head.

'I should think London solicitors would deal with all their business. Certainly we had nothing in this office. I'd never met either of them but I hear the girl was attractive. She was younger than him and I think he felt responsible for her.'

'What made her neurotic?'

'What makes any of us? There could possibly have been man-trouble, but nothing like that emerged and her brother would have known if there was. He put her nervous condition down to losing their parents in a car crash in the States. There was a considerable estate left, possibly the money cushioned the tragedy for him but maybe the girl was more vulnerable. But you haven't said what your interest is?'

Kemp pitched him the tale about his woman client who felt she might have once met Lucille Pearson, but even as he spoke he could see the scepticism in Tony's eyes.

'There was just one odd thing—' Tony continued to look bland—'That pond... She might never have been found if we'd not had all this dry weather. If the water level hadn't gone down so much she'd still be there.'

'But surely the brother would have searched for her at some time?'

Tony shrugged. 'He'd have no reason to search in the Forest. Remember she was supposed to be off to America. There was always the possibility of suicide in view of her record—she could have vanished anywhere.'

'There was no reason, then, to suspect foul play?'

'Why should there be? The evidence pointed to suicide. There was no mystery about it . . . Unless you're making one . . .' He gave Kemp a quizzical look. 'In your present line of work don't you thrive on mysteries? You used to discount them. Facts, you used to say, are chiels that winna ding.'

Kemp laughed. Tony was gently bridging a dangerous gap and he was grateful to him.

'It's not so bad. It's a living, and I get by...'

Tony became serious. 'Look here, Lennox—there are other jobs where you could use your talents... It seems such a waste. Besides, haven't I heard on the grapevine that you're applying for re-enrolment? I know these things take time, but can't you hurry the Law Society a bit?'

'I didn't apply,' said Kemp brusquely. 'I believe someone I did a favour for has put me up. I don't want to talk about it. Tell me, do you know this new partner of Robin Plender's, Benjamin Seft?'

Tony relaxed, having skirted a tricky subject.

'We don't know him well but of course he's about the district. Bit of a fireball, full of new ideas. The Plenders are very taken with him, he's quite an acquisition, I understand. Married to the daughter of Sir Herbert Smithers, the surgeon—you can imagine how that appeals to Betty.'

Kemp nodded, smiling but reserving judgement. When it came to social climbing Betty Plender had been a mere hill-walker compared to Muriel's capacity for the heights. He wondered if the same thought had passed through Tony's mind but the lawyer's next comment showed more relevant perception.

'Seft was Lucille Pearson's doctor, is that what you're getting at?'

'I'm not getting at anything,' said Kemp, rising, 'and I've wasted enough of your time, Tony. Thanks for talking about the case. While I'm in Leatown I might as well have a word with Lucille Pearson's brother.'

Tony gave him what is generally called an old-fashioned look.

'Do you think that wise, Lennox? Families don't much relish having private detectives nosing about in their tragedies. And coroners certainly don't welcome any aspersions on their verdicts.' Seeing Kemp's raised eyebrows, he went on: 'It's only for your own good, Lennox. I'm telling you not to meddle in what's over and done with.' His manner softened. 'Don't take it personally, old chap. So far as you yourself are concerned, please don't stay away from us so long in future. We won't bite you.'

The sun seemed to have become brighter when Kemp emerged into the High Street, or it may have been simply that a cloud had lifted from his spirit.

He went back for his car and decided it was time he saw Mr Leopold Pearson, particularly as everyone seemed to be warning him off. He knew he was being stubborn.

He took the narrow road out of Leatown up into the Forest towards High Beech. The roads were covered in fine dust. As he crossed Honey Lane Plain the hot August sun was slanting through the trees on the pinkish-brown straws of dried grasses and the crumpled plastic of ice-cream cartons. It was cooler when he entered the woods but darker where the trees crowded either side of the road.

He had driven that way so many times in the past that he automatically took great care to engage a low gear before the sloping bend where the ditch on the nearside was so dangerously close. He had met lorries racing down that corner, forcing up-climbing vehicles into the ditch, so he proceeded warily out of habit, and almost without thinking.

That wariness saved him from disaster. It was not from head-on the danger came. On the right-hand side there was a gap in the trees, an unused track which once led to a cottage long demolished. From that direction Kemp was suddenly deafened by the roar of an accelerator. He saw a glint of red and chrome in the sunlight, and braked hard as his car was struck a glancing blow which spun it into the ditch so fast that he didn't even get a glimpse of the other car, and as he wrenched at the steering-wheel to try to keep himself upright, all he heard was the screech of punished tyres and another tremendous snarling noise as it speeded off down the hill.

He climbed out carefully and stood back to look at the damage. The Morris had ended up with its nose firmly embedded in the clay bank, its wheels astride the ditch.

It had been no accident. The other car had been waiting for him in the gap, screened by the trees, then sent hurtling forward like a weapon of destruction.

With shaking hands he lit a cigarette, and looked round at the flickering shadows on the elm boles. He took a deep breath, and studied the chenille effect of lichen on bark, the purpose-built tracery of branches that gave every leaf its place in the sun, until his nerves steadied.

But annihilation had come too close for further meditation. There was no hope of moving his car, but he did know a garage in Leatown which specialized in pulling vehicles out of the Forest. As fast as the wardens dug ditches and put up embankments to prevent cars nosing their way into the quieter glades, the more enterprising courting couples found means of driving over and round them—with predictable results. The local garages, like modern wreckers on the shores of illicit love, charged a tidy sum to extricate their vehicles.

Kemp was hot, and not altogether steady on his feet after that shattering experience; to walk on up the hill to High Beech and Green Acres would exhaust such small store of athleticism as he had left. Far easier to go downhill to the garage. Leopold Pearson would have to wait.

SEVEN

THE TRAMP DOWN the dusty road might have bene-
fited Kemp's slightly assertive paunch but it short-
ened his temper as well as his breath. Fortunately the
garage owner recognized him, bore him no rancour
since he had been a good customer in the past, and
took it for granted that lawyers could have ups and
downs in their business as well as garage proprietors.
He listened to Kemp's edited version of the event in the
Forest and promised immediate first aid and hospi-
talization for the vehicle.

'By the way,' said Kemp casually, 'know anyone
around here who drives a large red car, powerful—
could be a sports model?'

Fred scratched his head. 'Don't you know the
make?'

'Only got a glimpse of it. A lot of power under the
bonnet.'

'The only person round here who drives a car like
that is Pearson—lives up High Beech way. If he's still
there—he's had a bereavement. But he's got a red
Morgan. It's been in here a couple of times in the last
six months for service.'

As Kemp left the garage he saw Robin Plender
across the street leaning over his car adjusting a wing

mirror. Funny what a small place Leatown had suddenly become.

The doctor crossed over to him.

'Lennox! Why, of all people... You've been away too long.' That was a reproach but unlike Egerton's it lacked sincerity. 'Betty will be glad to see you.'

Kemp doubted that, but he evaded the social issue by stressing he only had a short time in Leatown. Betty Plender had been a friend of Muriel's but Kemp didn't think they would have kept in touch. Robin Plender must have been conscious of the evasion also and would be content to leave it at that. Not a very deep fellow, Plender liked the appearance of things to be pleasant and for life to be lived at an emotional level as flat as a dinner table.

Now, standing in the street with him, Kemp was aware of the doctor's unease. 'I heard you were in the district,' he was saying. Kemp didn't ask how he'd heard. In fact Kemp said nothing, waiting for the other man to get round to it, which he finally did.

'Why'd you have to get Ben Seft's back up, Lennox?'

Kemp still said nothing.

'This awkward business of the Pearson girl...' Plender was fairly stammering, his eyes fixed on the wall of the café opposite as far removed from Kemp's gaze as possible. 'She was certainly a patient of the practice—a private patient actually, and there aren't many of these around here, but she was Seft's patient, not mine. I had seen her, of course—two or three times when he was away, and I'd been up at the house... You know the place, Green Acres?'

Kemp nodded.

'She suffered from some nervous disability—she was a very highly-strung young lady. Her brother was very concerned about her—as well he might be—but as I've said, she wasn't my patient.'

All right, Robin, Kemp felt like saying: I get the message, she wasn't your patient.

All he said was: 'Suicidal?'

'Well, of course I can't give you an opinion on that, Lennox. I didn't see her often enough to judge, nor was I treating her at all before the tragedy. I must accept what my colleague says. He's a good doctor, Ben Seft, and that was his diagnosis.' Robin's eyes continued to wander up and down the façade of the café as if picking holes in the plaster. 'No one has doubted his view of his patient—her brother even expressed his gratitude to Ben for the way he handled her... It wasn't easy...'

Kemp let him trail off into silence before saying gently: 'But you're not quite happy about it, are you, Robin?'

'Nonsense. I have implicit faith in Ben. I hope you're not going to cause any trouble?' His anxious eyes at last met Kemp's.

'Dr. Seft is a bit touchy, to put it mildly, on the subject of the late Miss Pearson,' said Kemp mildly.

'You've seen him, then?'

'Oh, come on, Robin, you know I have. He told you I was here.'

Plender sighed. 'Still as sharp as ever, Lennox? I can see you doing well in your new trade.'

It was not said in a nasty way; Robin Plender was not a small-minded man despite other limitations, but it sounded like a warning to Kemp to get the hell out and not presume too much on an old friendship which had never been based on other than social propinquity, and could well be too tenuous to stand the test of time and event. It could also be a hint that the medicos were, as was their custom, closing ranks against outsiders.

Aware of these nuances, Kemp changed the subject and told Plender he'd had an accident with his car in the Forest. It was a measure of Plender's relief that he immediately offered Kemp a lift home. Kemp demurred at thus taking up his time, but accepted a ride as far as the nearest Green Line bus stop.

During the next ten minutes he listened with growing wonderment to Plender extolling the virtues of his new partner. Seft had been with the practice for only a year but already had made a considerable impact, brought in new ideas, and of course his connections with the London hospitals and consultants were of inestimable value.

'He's a brilliant chap,' went on Robin with enthusiasm, 'we're damn lucky to have him.' One thing Plender could never be accused of, Kemp thought, was professional jealousy; it was not in his nature. But why, Kemp asked himself, is he giving me this glowing testimonial?

'Come and see us soon, Lennox,' Plender said on parting, 'I'll get Betty to give you a ring.' Reluctantly Kemp gave his telephone number; he had no particular wish to make social calls in Leatown, yet as the single-decker growled its slow way through the traffic he had time for reflection. There was something behind Robin's sudden friendliness, and he had protested too much his belief in the integrity of his colleague.

Was that all the trouble was, Kemp's own mishandling of Benjamin Seft? Kemp tried to rationalize. Doctors were inclined to bridle like old-fashioned spinsters if their diagnostic judgement was questioned. Perhaps that was all there was to it, and Robin had merely been trying to act the peacemaker.

But Kemp had more on his mind than the touchiness of the medical profession. He recalled, with sudden chill, that crash in the Forest. Why had he been headed off in no uncertain manner from Green Acres? He thought about the conversations he had had that day in Leatown; at the surgery, the police station, the solicitors' office. Word must have gone round fast that he was inquiring into Lucille Pearson's death. And someone had tipped off Leopold Pearson.

But why should a man he had never met engineer so violent a diversion?

EIGHT

THE GARAGE IN TRUE wreckers' tradition took three days and ransom in cash to repair what turned out to be only dented bodywork. Modern man without transport being like a knight without his charger, Kemp for these three days sulked in his tent, but the hours were not entirely wasted since he used them for some tentative investigations of his own.

When at last the car was ready he took off like a shaft from a bow for Green Acres. But the house displayed an unwelcoming aspect even to the sun; venetian blinds were closed eyelids drawn down over the windows and a board at the gate announced it was for sale. Kemp noted that it was his old friends Benson's of Loughton who invited inquiries.

He walked up the drive boldly. This time his entry was legitimate, he could be an invitee of the Agents. He might even buy the place if McCready paid him what he was worth for ten years or so.

Whatever else Malcolm Moss might be—and not too far back in Kemp's mind there was a nasty suspicion—he was undoubtedly an exceptional architect. The house had been designed for the plot, the terrain had come first and been given its scope. Consideration of the maximum views to the south and west had inspired the patio and long line of windows, so that the rooms on that side looked out at a wide expanse of sky, trees in the middle distance, and far away the dwarfed spire and tower blocks of the City rising from blue haze like Turneresque brushstrokes.

Kemp took a good look around. Money had obviously still been spent on maintaining the grounds but already the house had an abandoned air.

The receptionist at Benson's was not the knowledgeable young lady of his previous visit, possibly she had departed for W.1. where she belonged. Instead there was an eager youth, his hair fashionably long and elegantly placed. He was very, very talkative; he must have been selling houses for all of six months and disillusionment with the art had not yet set in.

A fine place, Green Acres, a real gentleman's residence; individually designed on a prime site. Had Mr Lennox seen it? Well, then, what a chance to buy! Yes, just on the market and inquiries already pouring in. Of course, it was so well known. Oh no, he didn't mean because of the tragedy—his face was pained suddenly as though he had been shown something repulsive. That had been an unfortunate business, an unhappy circumstance which had naturally led Mr Pearson to sell, and landed Benson's with this jewel of a property. He brightened up again. No, he had only meant that locally it had always been known as a desirable residence, both designwise and for its scenic value. And they were asking? Eighty thousand, but—he lowered his tone and crept closer as if to divulge a state secret—Mr Pearson did want a quick sale and might take less. Kemp asked if he might contact the owner. The pained expression returned: 'Oh no, sir,' he was reproved, 'negotiations are entirely in our hands. Mr Pearson left for America two days ago.'

Damn and blast. Kemp's angry frustration must have shown in his expression for he was instantly assured that Benson's were in a position to handle any prospective sale, and Mr Pearson's City lawyers could draw up an immediate contract.

'And they are?' asked Kemp nonchalantly. 'I may know them.'

Fortunately for Kemp, Benson's efficient salesmanship came to his aid. Rummaging in his files, the young man beamed: 'I see you're an interested purchaser, Mr Lennox, there's a note here from our Miss Beagley. You called in May about buying property in the Forest. Well, in that case I'm happy to give you the name of the Vendor's solicitors.'

'I'll have my own lawyers contact them,' said Kemp, very businesslike, having got the information he wanted. It seemed a pity to disappoint such an earnest young huckster however, so he went through the usual rigmarole of establishing further *bona fides* even if it did mean giving his own address before leaving. It would probably mean he would be deluged by letters and pressure to proceed but, short of actually signing a contract, he could play it along for what it was worth.

TONY EGERTON was aghast.

'You must be mad, Lennox. You're not really thinking of buying that place?'

'Why not?' said Kemp.

'But it's eighty thousand,' expostulated Tony. 'You haven't got that kind of money.'

'How do you know that?'

Tony raised a sceptical eyebrow but on getting no response other than a bland stare from Kemp, he sat back in his chair and became serious. He wagged an admonitory finger.

'You sold everything you owned, including your house, Lennox, to pay off those gambling debts of Muriel's... You even...'

'I know, I know...' said Kemp, with some irritation, 'I even dipped my grubby fingers in the till to do so. You don't have to remind me, Tony. But I've paid every penny of that Trust money back, and what I have now is my own.'

Tony Egerton remained unimpressed. Although Kemp had broken the ice of the past with him, without noticeable damage to either of them, he wondered now if the lifeline of old friendship would stand another tug, and decided to chance it.

'I have a client,' he said, 'who wishes to remain anonymous. Don't they all? Anyway, he's interested in buying Green Acres but he's a bit wary. Apparently Pearson has gone off to the States. You know how it is when the vendor and the purchaser aren't in a position to meet each other—there's always some uneasiness—you know the kind of thing: rats in the cellar, Gipsies camping in the grounds... All I want you to do is get a draft contract, copy entries, the usual preliminaries. Use the name Lennox, here's my address and telephone number. Let me know when you hear from Pearson's solicitors.

But Tony Egerton was not one to be taken in easily.

'You're still on about the Pearson woman, aren't you? Leave it alone, Lennox, if you've got any sense. You should know what old Trumball's like as coroner. He won't want anyone questioning that verdict—least of all you...'

Kemp looked bland astonishment. 'Why, Tony, all I'm asking you to do is routine conveyancing. I'll pay your fees. Just keep it under your hat, there's a good chap. And if the worst comes to the worst I might need a good solicitor!'

But Tony didn't laugh. 'You're playing with fire, you know. And at a time like this when you're up for re-enrolment... But you always were one to take risks. All right, I'll go along with the preliminaries, but it's on your head, remember...'

KEMP LOOKED AT his watch as he drove from Leatown; four o'clock, time for tea. Would he be offered any at Malcolm Moss's other house? He could think of no valid reason for such a visit, save that when trails diverge it's best to go back to the beginning.

As he rang the bell he heard her voice: 'I'll get it, Emma,' and she came to the door herself. She looked no different. She wore a sleeveless dress of some dull linen stuff and her arms were tanned. There was no moment of hesitation, surprise or non-recognition.

'It's Mr Kemp. How nice to see you.' She stepped aside, and he was in the hall and following her into the sittingroom.

Summer had brightened it, and there was chintz on the chairs, and bowls of roses standing about admiring their own reflection in pools of mahogany. The windows which had been velvet-curtained that night in May were now open to the garden, which was larger than might be expected in that road. It was a garden that had been in existence a long time, landscaped when the house was new, now full of colour, winding paths disappearing into shrubberies.

'Would you like some tea?' She went to the door and called, 'Emma, please bring two cups.'

Kemp found it hard to believe, but once they had commented on the weather and passed smoothly on to holidays, tea did arrive on a trolley with thin china, silver and lace. No cucumber sandwiches—but then she had not known he was coming. But there were macaroon biscuits and langues du chat so he couldn't complain. As always in the presence of Frances Jessica Moss, Kemp felt himself to have entered upon a slightly tilted dream world—somewhere between Alice's looking-glass one and Henry James's rosy vision of Edwardian England.

By the time tea was served they found themselves chatting easily like old friends unmet for years but now pleasantly re-encountered. They passed from roses, on which she was knowledgeable, to gardens abroad— they had just returned, she said, from Estoril. Did Mr Kemp know Portugal?

'Not this summer. I've been no further than Hackney Marshes. And it's Lennox, by the way.'

She smiled, but with a hint of impishness behind the eyes as if she too could recognize a leg-pull so long as it did not frighten away the civilities.

They discussed plays and films of which her cognizance was sketchy; and books, discovering that their reading stopped at much the same point. She slipped his first name unobtrusively into the conversation. They laughed a lot, finding common ground. Afterwards, Kemp couldn't remember why they laughed but the recollection of her laughter was to return to him again and again like memories of happy childhood.

She never asked him why he had come. She never inquired either into his personal life, or his work. Indeed, she did not appear to possess the inquisitiveness he had always assumed to be a natural trait in women. If her comments on the world were sharp and to the point, she yet lacked the scorn or malice usually attendant upon such remarks. It was as though she were a spectator at life's feast, and accepted what she was given uncritically and without reservation.

He could not make her out. He had come—and he certainly had no reservations about it—to probe into her marriage, to tease out some strand in the weave that would answer the questions buzzing at the back of his mind. All he got was the sweetly cloying odour of roses, roses all the way.

During the two hours he spent with her he felt more and more that he was moving, or being moved, within the pages of that Jamesian novel. The tranquillity of the room—from this part of the house there was no sound of traffic—lulled his normally acute senses. The peace of the garden beyond the open French windows, shading green on green into the shadows, the flowerbeds full blown with summer colour, Frances Jessica talking, not too little, not too much, drew out of him a response so natural and so pleasant that he found himself slipping into the illusion that here was perfection, here in this room the rightness of all things was being made plain to him. And he hadn't been drinking anything stronger than tea! It was an unnerving experience for one who was in the habit of seeing the world awry.

He did not know at what point he would have said why he had come, or if he would ever have said it. The initiative was in any event taken from him by a sound in the hall.

She rose, and Kemp's eyes followed the backs of her graceful pale brown legs as she went to the door.

'That will be Malcolm,' she said, calmly. 'No, please don't leave. I'm sure he would like to see you again.'

It was the first observation she had made that afternoon with which he could not agree.

Malcolm Moss came in, and kissed his wife, not effusively but not in any perfunctory manner either, it was an obvious daily ritual. Kemp, reverting to his usual sardonic self, wondered if he had kissed her so on his return that Saturday morning in May.

'You remember Mr Kemp?' she said, smiling.

In his face there was certainly surprise, and Kemp didn't think it was pleasant. Moss looked him very straight in the eye, and his expression held inquiry. He appeared to be in much better health than on Kemp's last visit.

Kemp decided to abide by the rule: never explain, and left it to Moss to ask openly what the hell he was doing there. Moss simply took refuge in a remark about the weather, and said the same as his wife had done: 'Please don't go.' He went over to a piece of furniture too old and beautiful to be a cocktail cabinet, and brought out bottles and glasses. 'What would you like to drink?'

Kemp said he would not take anything, and that he must be on his way, but Moss insisted, making unnecessary noises with the glassware.

'I'll take the tea-things out to Emma,' said Mrs Moss, wheeling away the trolley, 'Please pour me out a sherry, Malcolm.'

She closed the door behind her, and as soon as she had done so, Moss turned on Kemp.

'Why have you come here?'

'It so happened I was in the district, and I simply called.'

'I don't believe you. Leave us alone. It has nothing to do with you.'

He came over to Kemp. He was holding a glass of sherry and Kemp automatically took it rather than see it spilt, for Moss's hand was shaking.

'That girl your wife saw in this house in May—was that the Pearson girl?'

His face went white. For a moment his lips moved soundlessly. Then he must have got control of himself for after a moment he said quietly: 'I'll meet you somewhere. I can't talk to you here.'

'All right,' said Kemp and gave him the address of his flat. 'Is that your office?' asked Moss.

'No, it's my private address. When will you come?'

'Tonight—around eight o'clock?'

'Fine. I'll be there.'

Frances Jessica came back at that moment but gave no glance either of curiosity or question at either of them.

As they stood about, making the banal conversation of chance acquaintances, Kemp studied Moss. The long colourless face was expressionless, giving no clue to what he was thinking, but between himself and Frances Jessica there appeared to be complete rapport, excluding others.

Kemp downed his drink quickly, made his excuses and left.

NINE

LENNOX KEMP HAD USED Elvira before when he wanted notes taken unobtrusively. She was better than a tape-recorder. He called in at the council house where she lived with her mother and father—a circumstance out of tune with the times, but Elvira was an old-fashioned girl in a teenage environment; she was quite incapable of swinging with the Sixties.

He found her washing her hair. 'Have you got a date, then?' he asked. She shook her head which was turbanned in a towel. 'I wasn't going out, Mr Kemp.'

'I've got a job for you tonight. Someone's coming to see me and I want some notes taken. Could you manage it?'

'Sure. What time do you want me?'

Kemp arranged to pick her up at half past seven, and by eight o'clock she was sitting in his small kitchen, her notebook on the table, just behind the half-closed door. Elvira was very reliable; at the least hint of discovery her notes would be whisked into her bag and she would be making instant coffee.

Malcolm Moss arrived promptly. He had evidently given consideration as to what his attitude was going to be, and he was very composed. While he didn't ex-

actly sniff at Kemp's three-room apartment and in-
sipid decor, he was obviously unimpressed.

Kemp studied the man leaning back in the snuff-
coloured armchair opposite, and wondered what particular mesh of woven lies was about to be presented
to him. He always got depressed when people lied to
him, as they invariably did, although it was fifty per
cent of his job to listen to them. Lies, he thought, were
apt to be more boring than the truth, and there were
fewer surprises; cause and effect fitted neatly into each
other in a contrived predictable pattern whereas truth
was a careless blend of events lacking any perfection.
Besides, lying not only depreciated the teller; it also
belittled the recipient.

He was about to discover that Malcolm Moss was
good at lying, which gave Kemp his first real insight
into his character. Kemp was fairly expert in the craft
himself but he regarded it as something of a tool of his
trade; he could see no reason for its use by an architect.

It seemed that Malcolm Moss had been very much
upset by Kemp's call at his house in Crownberry Road.
He was most anxious, he assured Kemp, that his wife
should not be brought into this business at all. When
Kemp observed mildly that it was she who had brought
him into it in the first place, Moss scarcely concealed
his evident feeling that Kemp was a contamination
they could well do without.

'She was extremely worried about your where-
abouts for those—wasn't it five days, Mr Moss?'

'That has been quite satisfactorily explained to her.'

'But not to me.'

Moss looked at Kemp with speculation. If there had been a balloon above his head it would have spelled the word blackmail.

'It cannot be unknown to you, Mr Kemp, in your line of business to come across the kind of—er, infatuation—which unfortunately I had for the Pearson girl. I met her and her brother Leopold when I designed a house for them, and naturally I saw a great deal of them both. I liked Pearson, and I'm afraid his sister became fond of me. I'm not making excuses for myself—I did find her attractive. She was young and high-spirited . . . and somehow . . . different. You must understand that Jessica and I have always been very happy, but we lead a quiet life and we have been married for some years. A man gets—well, at my age—any man can get involved with a younger woman very easily.' He laughed nervously, 'I'm afraid all this must sound very commonplace. Man nearing forty and attractive young thing. Psychologists have plenty of explanations for it, I'm sure. I was flattered that she should fall in love with me, and for some time I was carried away by what I can only call infatuation . . .'

His cold grey eyes gazed reminiscently at Kemp's brown and yellow folkweave curtains as if he were reliving some illicit idyll. It was all make-believe, of course. Malcolm Moss, Kemp judged, had never been infatuated in his life and the idea that he could be carried away either literally or metaphorically was simply not on.

He was right in one thing, however. In Kemp's line of business, as he so nicely put it, Kemp did come across many men on the dangerous edge of forty who felt the pull of youth and responded with pathetic avidity to warm-limbed youngsters to whom the generation gap only applied to parents. So Kemp listened with understanding and murmurs of encouragement as Moss rolled out his magic carpet of fantasy.

' . . . And so you see,' he finished, 'I could not possibly have hurt my wife and broken our perfect relationship with this very sordid kind of thing.' He even managed a wry smile. 'It would only have upset her terribly, and anyway it was soon over . . . I had broken with Lucille, I had persuaded her that I had decided I could not leave Jessica. She seemed to take it quite well. And really, there was nothing in it—not what you think.'

Kemp raised his eyebrows. He hadn't given Moss any intimation of what he was thinking.

'Those five days, I mean. I stayed with the Pearsons at their house, but Leopold was there too.'

'You stayed out at Green Acres?'

Moss was startled. 'How do you know about Green Acres?'

Kemp shrugged, and lit a cigarette. Funny, Moss had never asked him any questions. He had come prepared to tell a tale and expected it to be believed.

'It was in the papers, Mr Moss. Green Acres was Lucille Pearson's home. Did her brother know of this affair?'

Moss frowned at the word as if it were in the same bad taste as Kemp's curtains.

'He certainly knew that Lucille had fallen in love with me. In view of her record of instability he was naturally very distressed. We talked about it, in fact, and it was because I knew that he understood that I thought it would be all right... After I left, I mean...'

'And of course she wasn't all right, was she?'

Moss ignored the interruption.

'Leopold was going to take her to America. They were going to leave almost immediately. I had no reason to believe they hadn't gone. You can imagine how shocked I was when I heard about her death... As you've gathered, Jessica and I have only this week returned from holiday, and we didn't see any English papers when we were in Portugal. I only heard about Lucille when I got back to the office and my colleagues were talking about it—because we'd designed the house for the Pearsons. I was dreadfully upset.'

For the first time Moss showed genuine feeling. His face was grey and his eyes anxious. There was appeal in them as he turned them on Kemp.

'For my wife's sake I cannot have my connection with this girl brought out now. You must see that, Mr Kemp, what a terrible thing it would be for her. Please believe me, I love her very much and cannot hurt her.

And I'm sure that you, Mr Kemp, now that you know her, would do nothing to ruin her happiness.'

Very perceptive, Mr Moss, thought Kemp. Who's using blackmail now?

Moss went on: 'She is such a gentle, good person. She has lived a sheltered life—could you shatter that security? It would break her heart...'

Kemp wondered if Frances Jessica's heart might not be made of sterner metal. Did Malcolm Moss really know his wife at all?

'When you heard of Lucille Pearson's death did you get in touch with her brother?'

Moss hesitated.

'I thought it better not to. It was such a shock, and anyway the inquest was over by the time I got back.'

He looked at Kemp very straight, very man-to-man. 'Would you have wanted to see the brother in these circumstances? Believe me, Mr Kemp, I'm not proud of my part in all this. I cannot but blame myself.' He almost hung his head; it was a great performance, thought Kemp, as he watched Moss take the last fence and gallop down the straight.

'And now what good will it do to rake the whole thing up? It can't bring Lucille back, and it would only ruin Jessica's life if she knew about it. I am left to regret the whole episode very bitterly, and believe me, Mr Kemp, it is on my conscience.'

There was altogether too much of the 'believe me, Mr Kemp' to be real. Kemp knew that all this high-falutin' nonsense about ruined lives and bitter regret wasn't on the same plane as real living. The language Moss was using smacked too much of the hushed two-syllabled rhetoric which people draft in their own minds in preparation for a difficult interview, or the funeral of someone not very well liked. The trouble with that kind of speech is that the woolly edges melt somewhere into near-truth so that it cannot be grasped like outright lies, and it is apt to affect the hearer so that he begins to talk the same way. But not Kemp. He had been to this place before, encountered all too personally that hazy field of principle and honour, and noble thought compared with iniquitous practice, the world of difference between the things men do and the things they say.

Malcolm Moss had relaxed. He went on talking some more in the same strain. He thought he had Kemp's compliance. Kemp must have nodded understandingly at some point—probably at the recurring motif, that marriage remained a sacred object, not to be sullied; infatuation on the other hand was like an illness, a fever, it would have its crisis and pass, the patient would recover. For an architect, Malcolm Moss had a fine way with words.

He was just unlucky in having Kemp around. He was treating him like a client to whom he had something to sell, which was to an extent true, but his assessment of Kemp was faulty. It was hardly Moss's fault. His wife had gone in desperation to an inquiry agent, associated in Moss's mind with those who dealt in the seamy side of divorce; obtaining statements of sordid adultery, rooting in wardrobes for feminine attire, peering into bathrooms for evidence of shaving gear, counting beds, cheating to get at hotel records, and finally handing over to a Judge the whole stinking mess, while standing there in the witness-box, a grubby figure in a shabby suit.

So he looked upon Kemp as a scruffy little man with a rotten job, and a rotten flat, and rotten taste in furnishings, and, not surprisingly, he made up his mind that Kemp too was rotten.

Kemp thought it was about time he justified such an estimation, and brought in the fireworks.

'And what did you tell your wife about those five missing days, Mr Moss?'

'I don't think that's really any of your business, Mr Kemp.' But he said it in a nice way as if, having established the proper relationship between them, Kemp was no longer worth being rude to.

'She accepted your explanation?'

'I was very open about it. I admitted the girl had become infatuated with me, and that I was embarrassed by it, that I didn't want a scene and that I went away with her to sort things out. I told her there was a brother who was in the position of guardian to the girl, that we were both concerned as to her mental health. In fact, I told my wife the truth, Mr Kemp.'

'But not about Green Acres?'

'It was of no importance. You do not seem to understand that there has always been absolute trust in our marriage. When I told my wife that it was all over, she never questioned me. She never asked the girl's name, or where she lived. There was no need for her to know, and now I'm glad that she did not know—and only you, Mr Kemp, can disturb her security, her happiness, her very life.'

So there they were, back again on that old tack.

'What time did you leave Green Acres?'

Moss looked at Kemp as if he were a building due for demolition.

'You know very well I was home on Saturday morning. Jessica rang up and told you.'

'I asked you when you left the Pearsons' house?'

Moss got up, and glared down at Kemp from his advantage of height.

'Look here, Kemp,' he said, dropping the civilities, 'I won't have you bothering either myself or my wife with your impertinent questions. If necessary, I'll see your employer and have you stopped. There must be some kind of code even in your business... Believe me, I'll do all I can to prevent you worrying my wife...'

'I believe you would. What time did you leave Green Acres? You and your pal Leopold couldn't have had much sleep that Friday night.'

Moss paced the room tight-lipped. He seemed to be contemplating several alternatives—whether to aim a punch at Kemp's head, fetch the police, call Mc-Cready or simply appeal to the better nature he doubted Kemp possessed. Kemp wasn't altogether surprised that he chose the last attitude. Moss had great faith in his powers of persuasion, and the other avenues would seem to be blocked. Just why, Kemp could hazard a fair guess.

'Leopold Pearson asked me to stay over Friday night because Lucille was much better, and as a matter of fact the three of us spent quite a pleasant evening. I was immensely relieved, it meant we could part as friends. Leopold had to go off on business early the next morning, and I left at the same time.'

'What, no fond farewell to Lucille?'

'She had gone to bed early, and was still asleep. I understood she was all packed to go to the States.' There was sweat now on Moss's forehead so Kemp turned the screw.

'Are you in the habit of carrying a bag of golf-clubs in the boot of your car?'

Moss was temporarily distracted. 'I don't play golf,' he said shortly. Then his eyes widened but he stared back at Kemp without a flicker in them. Which was a mistake; he should have at least shown surprise at the apparent inanity of the question.

There was a long silence. Kemp wondered which way the cat would jump.

When Moss spoke his voice was icy with contempt.

'I suppose in your trade making mountains out of molehills is a good way of making money. Well, it was a good try, Kemp. I suppose you fancy yourself as some kind of fictional detective.'

Kemp got to his feet. 'I've been insulted before, Mr Moss, but not often twice by the same person.'

There was no doubt of Moss's furious anger but he kept his control enough to sneer: 'Tough too, eh? Come now, Kemp, aren't you just looking for trouble? You're hoping there's money in it.'

Kemp took careful aim.

'A piece of that one hundred and fifty thousand you got for your Loughton branch wouldn't go amiss,' he said.

Malcolm Moss curled his lower lip in a scornful smile.

'As I thought,' he said coldly. 'You are quite despicable. People like you should be banned. I shall certainly see to it that my wife is not bothered by you again.'

Kemp wasn't sure whether he might have gone too far. He had been riled by Moss's attitude, and had allowed it to deflect him from his original purpose of sounding Moss out. He hadn't expected the other man to call his bluff in the blackmail stakes, and now it was too late as Moss turned on his heel and stalked out. Kemp waited a few moments before drawing aside the window curtains. Moss was still driving the white Rover.

Kemp waited until the rear lights vanished round the corner, then went into the kitchen where Elvira was already getting out the coffee mugs.

Her notebook lay on the table, the pages covered in the twigs and curlicues of her shorthand.

'I got it all down, Mr Kemp. I'll type it out for you in the morning. Shall I put the papers with the Moss file? I thought that was all closed.'

'Well, yes. Thanks, Elvira. Don't let Mr McCready see the transcript, though—might give him the wrong idea. By the way, what did you think of Mr Moss?'

Elvira stirred the coffee. 'I didn't see him, of course, but I thought he had ever such a nice voice, sort of low and cultured. It was like someone talking on the TV.'

'I meant what did you think of what he had to say?'

'He sounded ever so sorry about the girl. It was lovely, I thought, about not wanting to break up his marriage. Not a lot of men would be like that. Not sincere, like. And he couldn't help it if the girl fell in love with him—he sounded such a nice man...'

Kemp stared.

'What sort of books do you read, Elvira?'

She was confused by a question that didn't concern her everyday work. 'Oh, I dunno. I like romantic novels, but there don't seem to be a lot of them about, not with happy endings, and I don't like the other kind.' She went quite red. 'You know, Mr Kemp, sometimes I go back and read the things we had at school. We did *Jane Eyre* and *Cranford*, and I've gone and read them since, and—' she looked positively defiant—'I do like them. Don't you think life was more romantic then?'

Kemp hadn't the heart to disillusion her. As he drove her home he pondered on the ease with which Moss's story had gone straight to her innocent heart.

TEN

By LUNCH-TIME the next day Lennox Kemp was forced to realize by how much he had failed to take the full measure of this man, Malcolm Moss. Nemesis arrived on his doorstep in the presence of McCready himself. This was an unprecedented intrusion into Kemp's private life.

'Look here, Lennox,' he stormed, brushing aside such small civilities as the time of day and offers of coffee, 'this won't do. I've just had a Mr Moss on the phone to me complaining about you. And from what he's said he's got every right to complain. I understand you had his wife as a client—I've looked at the papers and the matter's closed. Now he tells me you've been out at his house bothering his wife. In fact he hints at something a great deal more serious—he hints at blackmail!'

Kemp said nothing, waiting for McCready to run out of breath and sit down. He finally flung himself into a chair, but he hadn't finished.

'It won't do,' he repeated, 'it simply will not do. I run my Agency on strictly professional lines, and I expect my operatives to behave within those lines. You know that. You, of all people, should know that we must have some ethics—otherwise we'd be out of business. The merest suspicion that we ever used our clients' confidences for our own ends—well, we might as well give up!' He glared at Kemp from bright little eyes, the very embodiment of the law; after all, he'd been a senior police officer until his retirement.

'It's not all in the file,' said Kemp calmly as he considered just how much to tell McCready. There were already aspects of the case which he could not handle alone. He needed time to think but by the look of his employer events seemed to be jostling too quickly upon each other for him to go on indulging in mere conjecture.

McCready had settled down, and was prepared to be nice.

'You know, Lennox,' he said, 'I've treated you fairly. I gave you a job when you needed one and I'll be honest with you, you've proved very useful to me, and up to now I've no complaints. We both know what was the cause of your troubles. You chose to take on your wife's debts—heaven knows you'd no need to, but you did. She was your wife then and I suppose you had your loyalties. She was a compulsive gambler—well, that was your affair, you married her. But taking money from that Trust fund—the Law Society had no option but to take the action they did... But that's all old history now. The choice was yours and the course you took at the time is something you have to live with...'

He paused, and Kemp didn't speak. Much as he might have respected McCready's strict Calvinist views, he didn't think this was the time or place for a moral lecture. He could see what was coming as the older man resumed.

'But this business of Moss, it could seriously damage your chances of being re-admitted. You know that. The Law Society are sympathetic—they would have been at the time if you hadn't been such a damn fool. But now—' he stared bleakly at Kemp—'if you put up any blacks like this thing with Moss, if it ever gets out, you haven't a hope in hell. And Moss will find out about you, never fear. From what he said to me on the phone he's out for your blood.'

Kemp sighed. Reflecting again on that crash in the Forest, he was rapidly coming to the conclusion that he had enough enemies, no point in McCready joining their ranks.

He said: 'What if I told you that I have good reason to suspect Malcolm Moss is a murderer?'

McCready's reaction was swift, and canny.

'Proof?'

'Nothing like it. So far only conjecture but based on facts which only I possess.'

'H'm.' McCready settled himself more firmly in his chair. 'Come on, out with it, what's all this about, then?'

Kemp told him straight, the whole series of events from Frances Jessica's visit to the office on the morning of that Friday in May up to the interview with Moss at Kemp's flat, but sticking to facts and omitting such conversations as he deemed too private or indiscreet.

'I've done some checking on Moss himself,' he finished, 'and he certainly seems to have led a blameless life, not even a traffic violation. He's never been in debt, his firm is sound. There's nothing amiss with his professional qualifications. He's been a clever lad, Liverpool College of Architecture, prizes all the way, joined this firm of Archer and Co. as a partner, took over on the death of Archer himself. Her story too checks out; they were married as she said in Folkestone, they've no children, they're very comfortably off but there's been no lavish spending. Then out of the blue this rubbishy story of the bright young thing and off goes this paragon of husbands!'

'And you think he murdered her? And Leopold Pearson helped him dump the body? Not a very brotherly act!'

'I saw two men,' said Kemp stubbornly, 'and they were both in Moss's car. It may have been someone other than Leopold Pearson. I've only got Moss's word that Pearson was in the house that night . . . Oh, and of course Pearson himself said so at the inquest.'

'So they were in cahoots?'

'And Pearson's gone back to the States. I'd like to have got a look at that man but I was stopped . . .'

'You think that crash was deliberate?'

'If you'd been there you'd have had no doubts.'

McCready rubbed his nose, and put on a shrewd expression.

'I don't like being taken for a ride by anyone,' he said, 'but if this man Moss is a murderer, then he's got a hell of a nerve coming to me with a complaint about you blackmailing him.'

'You need a lot of nerve to commit murder. And yet there's a whole lot of ends that simply don't tie up. If Malcolm Moss had a hand in the girl's death how come he had all these people fooled into thinking it was suicide, unless it was with the brother's connivance? There's something wrong at the Leatown end... It won't hurt the Agency if I look into that aspect.'

'It's my old friend Inspector Comfrey out there at Epping. Perhaps I'll give him a wee call.' McCready looked sagacious. 'But as far as you're concerned, you just keep away from that woman in Crownberry Avenue. I don't trust her any more than I trust her husband after what you've told me. Emerald rings instead of cash—what rubbish!'

Reverting once again to the old McCready, on that note he departed, leaving Kemp with much the same thought. Frances Jessica. Just where did she fit in? For a moment he was back in that sunny room where, like a great crystal bowl, a serene tranquillity transcended the everyday world of deceit and crime. Was it cracked, that bowl, like all other marriages? Coming back to the practicalities of time and place, for instance, where was this devoted creature on that Friday night in May when she should have been sitting anxiously by the telephone?

'Very open and straightforward evidence. She'd been on his books as a private patient only a short time. His records were in complete agreement with the reports produced by Mr Pearson—he'd diagnosed her as neurotic. He was an excellent witness, Dr Seft. Besides, he's the police surgeon—if he'd thought there was anything going on, he'd have reported it.'

'Can we check up on Leopold Pearson?'

McCready looked shocked.

'He's a law-abiding American citizen so far as we know. We've no reason to follow him up. We haven't even got an address, and anyway we've got no right to pry into his business affairs.'

It was at that moment Tony Egerton rang.

He was laconic. 'I've got that draft contract and copy entries. Pearson's solicitor has power of attorney to sell the property so the documents won't have to go chasing across the Atlantic.'

'Give me the entries,' said Kemp.

As Tony read them out, Kemp was astounded at the first name on the proprietorship register: Malcolm Moss, 72 Crownberry Avenue, N. 10. Moss had owned the land until May when it, and the house known as Green Acres built thereon, had been transferred to Leopold and Lucille Pearson c/o a business address in Lower Manhattan, as joint tenants.

Kemp scribbled a note and pushed the paper across to McCready who merely glowered at it.

'The price has been scratched out,' went on Tony. Kemp wasn't surprised; it was normal conveyancing practice before exchange of contracts, 'but it looks to me to be only four figures. Sounds fishy. Tax dodge, d'you think?'

'Or a gift. Keep it going a few more days, Tony—I might want to get a look inside the premises.'

'I'll stall them till I hear from you, but I still think you're raving mad, Lennox.' Tony rang off and Kemp turned to McCready.

'You've got pals in that American detective agency. That's Leopold Pearson's address. Come on, old chap, to hell with the expense, put a call in and see what you can get on the Pearsons—both of them. Say you're investigating a possible revenue fiddle, eh?' He could see that McCready's Scottish instincts were bothering him; it wasn't the ethics this time, it was the money.

'These inquiries are going to cost you, Lennox. Who else is going to pay us?'

Kemp grinned at him.

'Put it down to the cause of justice. If we prevent a miscarriage in that august female, we'll get thanked in kind if not in coin.'

McCready didn't look particularly impressed by this hypothetical argument, so Kemp became serious and explained.

'There's something deadly going on out there at Green Acres, and it involves money—a great deal of money. The sale of a prosperous business, the transfer of an expensive piece of property—all for love? All for a passing fancy which is what Moss would have me believe? And a body lying in the mud for months?

Solid identification, neat verdict, no further questions—except by me, and I'm headed off in no uncertain manner, while big brother skips the country? I'm the joker in the pack. Only you and I know what I saw that night, so why's everybody got so jumpy, tell me that?'

McCready only grunted, but at least he did take the scrap of paper with him when he finally left.

ELEVEN

THE HOME OF THE Fosters, a picturesque timbered
cottage on the edge of Honey Lane Plain, was rose-
clad and rustic enough on the outside to charm the eye
of visitors to the green rides in the Forest nearby, but
the inside was lamentable. They were a feckless lot, the
Fosters, as Lennox Kemp well knew. His previous
dealings with them had at one time covered a fairly
wide spectrum at the lower levels of the judicial sys-
tem.

He had supported the parents through various
stages of truancy proceedings—children sent off to
school in winter tended to creep back to the roaring
fire in Gran's kitchen, while in summer they preferred knocking about in the woods to the scholastic
duties which might overtax their little minds. As they
grew up the lads took to poaching and the odd pilfer-
ing from building sites; their entrepreneurial genius in
taking-and-driving-away was only marred in the execution by a habit of leaving the vehicles outside one of
the Forest pubs also frequented by the local consta-
bulary. Tirelessly Kemp had pleaded mitigation in
front of weary magistrates who'd seen it all before and
must have known every freckle on the boys' fore-
heads. The growing girls weren't much better; they

succumbed to other frailties, to the despair of social workers assigned to their welfare.

Old Mrs Foster was a proper Gammer Gurton, pure country Essex but wise to the ways of London's East End. Apple-cheeked even in age, she ruled her family with sharp tongue and hard hand. Her daughter-in-law Violet—and well-named—had worked for Kemp and his wife Muriel in their spacious days. Our Vi, as she was called, was a thin wire of a woman, flattened into the background by her boisterous, no-good husband and the noisy brood of their innumerable children. But she had had a daughter, Angela, a whining string-haired child whom she sometimes brought with her to the Kemps'. What age would she be now? Kemp wondered. About eighteen—old enough to have found a place in service at Green Acres.

He went over in his mind what he had learned from McCready who had seen her statement.

She had worked for the Pearsons for three months until May. Yes, she had liked working for them. No, she'd seen nothing unusual except that Miss Pearson wasn't well. She'd been given her wages and holiday money on Friday, May 12, and she'd not been back there since. She had not mentioned anyone else stay-ing at Green Acres in that last week, thought Kemp somewhat bitterly, but then she'd not been asked. If she had seen Moss, she apparently wasn't saying. She had been upset when the body was identified as Miss Pearson. Miss Pearson had been good to her, given her dresses and things. Yes, she had liked Miss Pearson, who was often ill and stayed a lot in her bedroom. Yes, she'd seen her out riding, and sometimes walking in the Forest. No, she'd not seen anyone with her on these occasions. Yes, she knew Miss Pearson's favourite bag, a big red leather shoulder-bag. Yes, she'd helped Miss Pearson pack to go to America, she'd cleared out all her clothes and personal belongings. End of statement.

It was Violet Foster who answered Kemp's knock this early September evening. Her sallow face registered a dull recognition and she let him in, murmuring incomprehensible words about how kind it was of him to call, Gran would appreciate it, they were all in such a state. As this was a normal circumstance with the Foster family, Kemp thought nothing of it and followed her into the dark kitchen.

The evening meal was being cleared by two of Violet's girls while husband Ron and the boys lounged around the fire, feet on the fender, jeans tight about their hips. It all seemed as it had always been in that house, although somehow unnaturally quiet. There was no sign of Angela.

Gran was at the sink, up to the elbows in greasy water, but when Kemp went over to her she turned, wiped her hands on a tea-towel and shook his hand. 'Nice of you to come, Mr Kemp,' she said, 'in our trouble.'

Violet silently produced a chair. She was sniffing into a rolled-up handkerchief. Kemp sensed misfortune, a deeper misfortune than usually afflicted a family not often blessed with fair weather. 'I am so very sorry,' he said inadequately.

'You've heard about our Angie, then?' Ron asked, fumbling for a cigarette. Kemp held his breath, and barely nodded. To gain time he took out a packet and offered them round. It was like a wake; in the corner by the fire one of the girls was crying. 'Not the details,' said Kemp cautiously. 'What happened?'

It was Jamie, the middle boy and the brightest star in the Foster galaxy, who told him that Angela was dead. Kemp closed his eyes for a second as the shock registered.

'Last night it was,' said Jamie. 'She had an accident. Came off her bike on that Claypit Hill. She hit her head... Fractured her skull, like—that's what they told us at the hospital.'

'It weren't a bike,' put in Ron. 'One of these moped things—never was safe.'

'Japanese sewing-machines,' muttered one of the boys, 'she never learned to ride it proper.'

'You'd have been glad of the chance,' Jamie rounded on him. 'Our Angie was doin' all right for herself. She'd been ridin' it long enough...'

'It were a waste of good money, and now look where it's got her!' Poor Ron was caught between anger and tears.

Kemp got up and put his arm round Violet's thin shoulders which were shaking. He knew she'd worked her fingers bone-thin to try and raise and control her spirited offspring. She hasn't deserved this, he thought savagely.

'Is there anything I can do for you, Vi?'

She shook her head.

'It was nice of you to come, Mr Kemp. She didn't suffer any, they said. She was dead when they got her into the hospital...' She put away her handkerchief. 'Would you like a cup of tea?'

Kemp said he wouldn't stay. In their incoherent grief they had all assumed he had come to offer his condolences, but further words stuck in his throat. The atmosphere in the kitchen was stifling, heavy with the burden of thoughts and feelings unable to be voiced. Sorrow was the worse for being inarticulate.

He said quietly to Jamie: 'I'm really terribly sorry about Angela. Perhaps I can help in some way. Would they mind if you came out for a pint—we could have a talk.'

The boy's face brightened; obviously he would be glad of any excuse to be out of the house. 'You don't mind, Gran, if I go out for a bit with Mr Kemp? Mum?'

No one seemed to mind his going.

Old Mrs Foster shook hands with Kemp again as if any human contact might be a comfort. 'That's right,' she said. 'Take the lad out of here—it's been hard on him. He was that fond of our Angie. We can't even bury her until there's been this inquest... but Matron at the Cottage said that'll be soon over. Then there'll be the funeral... Folks don't know how to mourn proper these days...'

There seemed to be no adequate reply to the Grandmother's comment, encompassing as it did the fleetness of time, the perils of modern machines and a whole line of buried children, so Kemp was silent as Violet showed him to the door. Jamie followed him out.

'We'll just go down to The Woodman,' Kemp said to him. 'Get in the car and I'll take you.'

It was only five minutes' drive and nothing was said until they were in a corner of the bar, and Jamie Foster had had a good swig at his beer.

Kemp reckoned he would now be about twenty-four. When he had been in his teens Kemp had managed to get him a suspended sentence on some long-forgotten charge, and Jamie had been grateful.

'There weren't no one else in the accident to Angie, Mr Kemp. She'd been up at The Oak. She'd been goin' there a lot, what with working up at Pearsons', like... Don't want the family knowin', but I guess she'd had a bit to drink. She couldn't take it, see? She just came off on the hill, knocked her head on the road. Of course she didn't wear no helmet, waste of money, she said, and she'd only on a silly woolly cap. She'd have lain there and died, I reckon, but doctor's car come along. An' he took her to the Cottage hospital 'cos it's near, like, and she just died there.'

'Local doctor? Dr Plender?'

'Naw,' said Jamie, 'there's a new chap since your time, Mr Kemp. Dr Seft. He's our doctor now anyway, so he knew right away who she was, and afterwards he come and told us. Terrible shock it was for Mum. Like that time with our Georgie, remember?'

Kemp remembered. Young George had skidded on a pushbike, stolen of course, which had no brakes, but he was lucky and was only concussed. He made a splendid recovery and in no time at all was in a detention centre for causing actual bodily harm to one of his mates. Certainly Vi Foster had had her troubles.

'You straight now, Jamie? Got a job?'

'Yes.' Jamie was surprisingly enthusiastic about work, which in that family was rare. Perhaps he took after his mother. 'I'm with Chard the builder—and no, thanks, no more police stations for me.'

'Good lad. I'm very pleased about that. I gather Angela had a job up at Green Acres?'

'That's right. Only for a while though 'cos they went off to America. Well, not really—at least she didn't, Miss Pearson, I mean. Angie was fair upset over that. Miss Pearson was good to her...'

'So I gathered. She gave her things, didn't she?'

The young man suddenly looked uncomfortable. He was about to speak, then stopped. It struck Kemp that Jamie was struggling with something on his mind. Kemp decided to give him time.

'Another one, Jamie?' Kemp stood up.

'Yeah, don't mind if I do.'

Kemp took his time at the bar, and when he came back to the table Jamie was staring down at its puddled surface. He took a long drink, and seemed to have come to a decision.

'Look, Mr Kemp, I don't want to get into no trouble—I had enough of that in the past. I reckon you're the best person to tell... You know the fuzz and you know when to keep your mouth shut. Can I tell you something that'll go no further?'

There were extenuating circumstances and anyway Kemp's sense of honour wasn't too elevated, so he nodded.

'Well... Like I said, our Angie had been taking to drinking—it were one of the fancy ways she'd learned up at that Miss Pearson's—martinis and gin and all that, stuff she weren't used to. She got pretty worked up when they found that body, and she was a bit excited, like. After the inquest was over Angie went out on a real blinder with some yobs that come up from Hackney. Anyway...she gets in real late. Gran and Mum, well, they didn't know what was goin' on, not about the amount of drink, like...Angie's practically delirious, and shoutin' all over the place. Seems she was goin' down with the 'flu on top of it all, see, so Mum she calls the doctor, so nothing's said about the drink and Angie's sent off to bed. I'd been the only one in that night 'cept for Gran and Mum, so next morning I told Angie off right and proper for gettin' tipsy, and for bein' such a stupid little git, raving away like she did. She wanted to know what she'd been saying, and I told her.'

Jamie stopped and took another long drink. Certainly since Kemp had first known him he'd lost all of his taciturnity. The beer was helping, and all Kemp had to do was listen.

'Angie'd been sounding off a lot of stuff about green stones and the tall man. She kept on about these green stones, and this man, and that she wasn't to say nothing and she would have money. When I told her what she'd been raving about she got all frightened, like, and cried and said I wasn't to tell no one, and that it was just that Miss Pearson had a secret and she'd given Angie money not to say anything. Well, we all knew Miss Pearson had given Angie money when she got her notice, it was far more than she need have for the short time she had the job. Angie spent it on clothes and the Honda. It doesn't seem to matter now she's dead anyway...'

As he said the words they seemed to bring his sister back, and the tears came, filling his eyes and running down his cheeks. Kemp gave him a cigarette and lit it.

'Sorry, Jamie. Can you go on?'

'I'm OK.' He rubbed his face and drew smoke in fiercely. 'It's like this, Mr Kemp... Angie said Miss Pearson had given her some dresses and things. Well, that morning Angie told me to go in a drawer in her room and bring out a green scarf—she were in bed with 'flu—and she said she didn't want the scarf any more. She said I was to keep it for her but I weren't to let anyone else see it—I was to keep it safe for her. So I did what she said. I went to the drawer and got out the scarf—it were all rolled up, like. All our Angie said was, You keep it, Jamie; so I just shoved it in my tool kit—you know there ain't anywheres in that house you can hide anything. But I took it out today 'cos it reminded me of Angie—' Jamie's eyes were again wet, and he wiped at them angrily—'and it's got a knot in one corner—look, Mr Kemp, I've got it right here.'

He struggled with the pocket of his jeans, and brought out a crumpled piece of green silk. It had 'Hermès' printed on it, and it was knotted in one corner. Jamie pulled at the knot and out on to the beer-stained table rolled a green stone which caught the bar lights and flashed them back in pinpoints of virescent fire. Kemp picked up the stone and turned it between his fingers.

'That ain't just any old green bead, is it?'

'No, Jamie, it isn't. You and I know this is an emerald and probably worth a great deal of money.'

'You're not kidding. But I can't keep it, Mr Kemp. Angie never said nothin' about it at the inquest—never said anything to the fuzz—but she knew it was there all right in that scarf. She was frightened that morning when she knew she'd got drunk the night before and talked about the green stones. That's why she wanted me to keep the scarf for her... But Angie wouldn't steal, Mr Kemp. Miss Pearson must've known when she give it to Angie what was in the scarf. She meant our Angie to have it. It were Angie's by right, weren't it, Mr Kemp? You know all about the law—weren't it Angie's property?'

Kemp could see what Jamie was getting at. If it had been indeed a gift would *donatio mortis causa* hold water? A gift made in expectation of death. Had Lucille Pearson anticipated death—by her own hand?

Despite the hot air in the little bar, Kemp felt cold. Too many deaths sewn up and never to be questioned. Was someone playing a very clever game? So far Kemp felt he had been dealt only the wild cards.

Having handed over the gemstone, Jamie seemed relieved.

'I'm glad to be rid of the damn thing. If it had anything to do with Angie's death then I never want to see it again. I wish she'd never gone up to those Pearsons. She weren't really like that, you know, drinking and dressing up and trying to talk posh—that weren't our Angie at all until she went up there...' Jamie was gulping down the last of his beer and not caring that his tears were falling.

Kemp could not tell him that it was all in the process of a girl growing up. Jamie was thinking of the kid sister who climbed trees with him and raced him across the green. In fact too, Kemp had a sudden remembrance of the girl and was not ashamed of the hot prickling behind his own eyes. But his were tears of anger. Lucille Pearson had only been a name to him, and a stranger. Angie Foster was the child who used to come into his kitchen and was fed biscuits and lemonade by Muriel. He saw her now as he once had done, sitting on a step in the sun crying because she'd broken a sandal strap. He had mended the little dirty shoe, and she'd dried her tears and run off in a squeal of giggles.

How did the lines go?

A cheel's full joys, an' a cheel's short sorrows,
Wi' a power of faith in girt tomorrows...

Kemp found himself surprised by being engulfed in a flood of rage.

He had difficulty keeping his voice under control as he said to Jamie: 'You've done the right thing. Now you must trust me. I have a jeweller friend who'll give us a valuation on this stone and keep it in his safe until I've solved the problem of its ownership.'

But when he left Jamie outside the darkened household of the Foster family and drove back to his flat his thoughts were in chaos and were concerned with harder things even than the emerald wrapped in green silk and now lying snug in his pocket. He was thinking of another stone in a gold ring that had flashed similar green brilliance as the May sunshine caught it, the first time he had ever heard of Malcolm Moss.

TWELVE

JOE CROHN RARELY SHOWED surprise, but his eyebrows twitched when Kemp unrolled the green scarf on
his dented deal counter among the accumulated trash.
The emerald winked at them both like a courtesan
caught in a rough house. Joe swept the plated spoons
and tarnished medals to one side, and gave the stone
its place. He picked it up with something approaching reverence, and applied his eyepiece.

'Don't know where you get 'em, Lennox. First you
bring me that ring—first-class stone in second-rate
setting. Then you bring me this! You found the treasure of the Indies?'

'It's that good?'

'Where'd you get it? Oh, all right—you're not prepared to say. Your Agency clients must be stepping up
a class!'

'It's private,' said Kemp hastily.

'Well, I didn't think you got it on the National
Health,' said the jeweller sarcastically.

'Keep it in your safe for me, Joe, scarf and all, until I come in again.'

Kemp sauntered out of the shop confident that he
had been right; these were stones of exceptional qual-

ity. Just how many had been set for Frances Jessica's birthdays and how had this single beauty gone astray?

Because she was in his mind, as if on cue she reappeared. A call from Elvira brought Kemp hurrying to his office: Mrs Moss was once again in the waiting-room cooling her well-shod feet on the shabby strip of carpet, and asking for Mr Kemp.

It was like a re-run of her May visit save that now she wore a light linen coat, a covering as inconsequential as the last one. Also, Kemp this time knew her better—or thought he did.

'And what can I do for you, Mrs Moss?' He was determined to be cool. The assortment of random facts he had collected would remain secure in his head unless he was obliged to use them as trading stamps.

'You must think me very foolish, Mr Kemp.' She fiddled with the clasp of her handbag—unfashionable shape but good lizardskin—and he noticed on her finger a twist of gold. It was a different ring and a more modest stone but it had the same arrogant green glint in it.

'No one who comes to McCready's Agency can be entirely foolish,' he said politely. They were not on the footing now of rose bowls and good books.

She had sensed his hostility and adapted herself accordingly; her antennae must be very finely tuned.

'This time I can pay you properly.' She had got the clasp open and produced two five-pound notes. 'I want you to find Malcolm.'

'What, again?' The whole scenario was becoming too ridiculous. He took out his cigarettes and offered her one. 'Oh, I forgot, you don't smoke.'

The light hazel-brown eyes were pleading with him to take her seriously. They looked devoid of guile but Kemp was taking no chances.

'Don't tell me there's been another elopement,' he observed with calculated flippancy.

Mrs Moss gathered up her gloves and rose swiftly.

'Mr Kemp—you asked me to call you Lennox but I cannot bring myself to do so now—you are treating me in a frivolous manner, and therefore you cannot help me...'

She was almost at the door when Kemp leapt from his seat. He took her arm and led her back to the chair beside his desk.

'I'm sorry,' he said, brushing the hair from his temples and aware as he did so that sudden exertion wasn't good for his blood pressure, either that or it was the effect of this Circe of a woman. 'I was unsympathetic. Perhaps you really do need my help. What has happened?'

She told the sequence of events slowly as if feeling her way, her soft voice steady.

She had not seen her husband since Monday morning when he left the house for the office as usual. It was now Wednesday and he had not returned home. She had phoned Archer and Co. and been told that Mr Moss had left there at midday on Monday, saying he had to visit a client, and he had not been back to the office since. They were also somewhat concerned since he had appointments over the two days which he had not kept.

'What do you expect me to do?' asked Kemp when she had finished.

'Find him.'

Just like that. Produce her husband like a rabbit out of a hat.

'If, as seems all too likely, his present disappearance has to do with that affair in May,' he told her deliberately, watching her face to see the effect of each word, 'then I have to know what explanation he gave you then for his absence.'

'Yes, of course.' She settled her handbag in her lap, and fixed her eyes on the mournful Labrador puppy in Kemp's animal charity calendar as if she was about to offer him a biscuit. The pose, for such it seemed to be, kept her face tilted away from him so that Kemp could see the flush that ran along her jawline. 'Malcolm told me exactly what had happened. There was this brother and sister for whom he designed a house, and during the building operations he saw a lot of them, and they all became very good friends. The sister—I gather she was young and rather highly-strung—well, you'll remember I described her to you? Anyway, unfortunately she fell in love with Malcolm. Although he did not return her affection he was concerned about her... That evening she came to the house she was on the verge of a mental breakdown, and he simply had to go away with her as he was afraid she would harm herself if he did not go with her. Malcolm stayed at their house during that week as a favour to the brother until the girl was calmer and in proper care. But Malcolm had promised that he would not speak of the matter to anyone—for there were elderly parents to consider, and the brother wanted to keep the girl's condition quiet... And, Mr Kemp, I know my husband. Loyalty means a great deal to him. If he gave his word to his friend then he wouldn't break it.'

'I see,' said Kemp, reflecting that as a Victorian novelette it would certainly commend itself to a girl like Elvira. But Mrs Moss? Well, it had all the right ingredients to appeal also to a sensitive woman; the oath to a friend, the keeping of faith, the concealment from parents, the brotherly care—secrets with just a hint of madness, Mrs Henry Wood couldn't have done better.

Mrs Moss sat waiting for Kemp's reaction. Was he supposed to be a filmgoer mesmerized by events shown on a screen?

'Did you know their name was Pearson? Leopold and Lucille Pearson?' Looking into her widened eyes as she turned her head towards him, he saw nothing but bewilderment, so he went on: 'The brother and sister your husband told you about—their name was Pearson.'

'He never mentioned their names. It wasn't important to me so I never asked. But how do you know their name?' She didn't appear startled but a small frown had creased the skin between the spaced eye-brows and sudden pallor showed up the light scattering of cinnamon freckles. The transformation grew as Kemp watched her. She looked tired, dusty and no longer young.

'Had you ever heard their name before?' Kemp's voice came out harsher than he had intended, and her reply was quick and equally sharp.

'No,' she said defiantly. Defiance didn't come naturally to her so that the curl of her lip was like the stubborn petulance of a child.

'Do you know a property called Green Acres?'

'No,' she said again, gazing at the wall in front of her. Kemp studied her averted face and the tide of red rising along her neck. 'Look at me,' he rapped out.

She did turn her head towards him but her eyes had dropped, searching the top of his desk as if for answers.

Kemp waited, but when she still said nothing he got tough with her as he might have done with a recalcitrant witness in court.

'Where were you that night when I phoned you, that Friday night in May?'

But the woman could still match him; she had had long experience. 'You won't believe me, Mr Kemp...'

'Try me.'

'I was out...'

'Out where exactly?'

It took time. She looked round the office, she even looked out of the window and his gaze followed hers.

The Harp girl was already curling brown at the edges—the summer had been hard on her as it had been on all of them.

'I found Malcolm's office keys...' She finally got round to it. 'I thought there might be something there that would explain his going away with that girl. Perhaps she worked in the firm, I thought. I went to Archer and Co. that night. I used the keys and let myself into the office...'

'And what did you find?'

'I didn't find anything, Mr Kemp.' Her eyes seemed to have grown larger, the dark smudges under them more pronounced, and the bloom had left her cheeks.

It was possible that she had not seen the file, but if she had then the photograph was there and the name and address.

'Did you go out to Green Acres that night, Mrs Moss?'

She shook her head.

'I hired a taxi to take me to Islington. I waited until the office closed. It must have been about six o'clock. I didn't find anything... I came straight home. Presumably I missed your telephone call. What time did you ring?'

But Kemp wasn't going to give her that way out so he said nothing, and let her go on.

'I didn't want to keep the taxi waiting. I felt like...like a burglar... Going into my husband's office... So I had to take public transport home—it must have been quite late when I got back...'

'It must have been, Mrs Moss. It must have been after midnight.'

She recovered quickly. 'Why did you phone me that night, Mr Kemp? Had you found out where Malcolm was?'

But Kemp was not to be drawn. All he said was: 'And the next morning your husband returned, and all was well, eh?'

She nodded.

'But this time it's different. Please believe me, Lennox. I really am worried. Malcolm wasn't himself over the weekend. He was preoccupied, and didn't talk very much. There was an airmail letter came for him on Saturday and it seemed to upset him. I had picked it up in the hall with the rest of the post. I think it was from America. When I asked him about it he just said it was from an old client, but...'

'Well, it wasn't from his girlfriend, Lucille Pearson. She's dead, you know.' Kemp brought it out brutally. He had grown tired of her equivocation, the ease with which she had switched back to 'Lennox' as if recalling the ambience of that sunny afternoon; he was tired too of her influence on his mind, his inability to break the enigma of what was either absolute honesty or artful duplicity.

Her gloves had dropped from her lap, and her hand was trembling at the edge of her open mouth.

'Your husband didn't tell you that, did he?'

'What happened?' she whispered.

'She's supposed to have committed suicide probably sometime in May. It's possible it happened about the time your husband was out at their house. She's supposed to have drowned herself in a pond near Green Acres—that's out in Epping Forest, if you didn't know... The body was found a few weeks ago, and identified by her brother Leopold.'

If he had hoped she would go down under his hard-hitting tactics he was to be disappointed.

'Malcolm couldn't have known! We've been away. Oh, that poor girl! No wonder Malcolm and her brother were so concerned for her... She really was mentally ill, then?'

Frances Jessica had rallied so fast to the defence of her husband that she drew all the force out of Kemp's attack. She bent down and picked up her gloves. The effect of the small action was to bring the colour back into her cheeks, and hide the expression in her eyes.

Her voice now was eager. 'Oh, don't you see? If Malcolm has only just heard this terrible news it might explain why he has gone away for a few days. He must be dreadfully upset... Perhaps he wanted to be alone. He would not have wanted me to know anything about it... Do you think that's possible, Lennox?'

And it's possibly my pretty poster girl will slide from that wall, shimmy across the street and give me a big kiss, thought Kemp wearily. Everyone seemed to have such good plausible reasons for their behaviour, no matter how outlandish.

'Your Malcolm knew the girl was dead when he came to see me. Did he tell you, by the way, that he'd warned me off?'

She had the grace to blush. How the hell does she make that rose colour come and go at will, he wondered.

'He did say something about it... He didn't want me to be reminded of that incident in May.'

'Incident? You were damned worried that time!'

'But it's all been explained.' She thought for a moment then she said, slowly as if feeling her way. 'Perhaps that letter was from the brother. Malcolm told me that when it was all over they might go back to America. No wonder he was so disturbed on Saturday when the letter came... I think he may have gone away simply to have a few days to get over it...'

'Have you looked for this letter?'

'Yes, I did look, but he must have taken it with him. We're not in the habit of locking things away.'

'You mean you have no secrets from each other?' The sceptic in Kemp made him smile as he said it so that the words lost any sting.

Her eyes were looking past him, into some distance of her own making.

'I did not say that,' she replied steadily, 'In a good marriage there are many secrets.'

It was a philosophy new to her listener. He pushed the banknotes across the desk towards her with the back of his hand.

'Then perhaps when your husband returns this time he'll have another explanation handy, Mrs Moss. There's nothing more I can do for either of you.'

He got up and held the door open, dismissing her.

For the first time in their ambivalent relationship he saw her drop her guard. The hesitation was brief as she smoothed the fingers on her gloves, slid the strap of her bag over her wrist, and walked slowly towards him. Her mouth was slightly open over those absurd doll's teeth, as if she were about to speak and desperately wanted to. But the moment was gone, even as her eyes seemed to flicker in appeal, or panic, as she passed him. It might have been just a trick of the light.

Exasperated, he flung himself into his chair and tried to think. What had she really come to tell him? Not simply that the wayward husband was off again, but that he had received a letter from America—and it wouldn't be from Alistair Cooke. The elusive Leopold Pearson. Had she really never heard of the Pearsons?

Kemp tried to envisage what might have happened if she had seen the photograph in the file. What would have been a normal wife's reaction? Kemp didn't much like the picture rising unbidden in his mind. A taxi which she said she didn't keep—but a taxi could have taken her further out, a helpful taxi-driver could even find the house . . . It was possible that more people than he already knew had converged upon the Forest the night he had watched Moss's car. No wonder the hornbeams had been sniggering—they'd had front row seats.

Kemp tried to shrug off the unwelcome thoughts but they lingered, growing in strength as he reluctantly fitted the pieces together, and, like four-in-the-morning thoughts, they brought with them other, nastier ideas. What if the Mosses were in it together—husband and wife united in the destruction of the pale blonde who threatened their perfect marriage?

Kemp swore, and began again.

All right, Frances Jessica had seemed to show horrified surprise at hearing of the death of Lucille, but the sad news had also subtly cheered her. That letter which had come for her husband: did she really imagine it had been written by the deranged girl Malcolm had told her about and that he was still under her spell, or was that only what she wanted Kemp to think? He wondered if she had bothered to check her husband's passport as she had done the first time, in that open house where they never locked things away from each other but kept their respective secrets tight-locked in their own bosom?

He looked at those damned banknotes she'd left on his desk, made up his mind and stuffed them in his pocket.

Whatever she was, this Frances Jessica who had taken possession of his mind, and was perhaps also—because she had found it vacant—rapidly taking a tenancy of his heart, she had paid him.

THIRTEEN

HIS TELEPHONE WAS RINGING when Kemp returned to the flat. He was mildly surprised to hear Betty Plender's high girlish voice inviting him to dinner. So, Robin was still mending fences? Kemp waited as Betty said her piece: she was delighted that Lennox had surfaced after so long, that Robin wanted—indeed so did she—to see him again, would Friday be all right?

Kemp said yes, his evenings stretching blankly ahead into the foreseeable future as free from engagements as they were from any other anticipatory joy, he could manage Friday.

'Eight o'clock, then. Wear something comfortable.'

She rang off, leaving him with the illusion that conventional mores in Leatown had not greatly changed since he and Muriel had lived there. The ladies had invariably outdressed each other in happy competition at Plender dinner parties, letting their men relax in shabby casuals so as not to dim their feminine glory. Kemp wasn't sure that he could stand going back over that lost ground again. But he told himself he could surely by this time stand aside, the memories had all been swept into heaps of dead leaves and burnt, no smoke to sting the eyelids.

He shook his head to free it from the dust of reminiscence, and thought about Malcolm Moss. He ought at least to make some effort to trace once again that will-o'-the-wisp who would doubtless turn up anyway with another fairytale to add to his wife's collection.

But, as in all fairytales, there is a darker side: the last time Malcolm Moss went missing from home a girl died; now he had been gone since Monday, and on Monday night in the Forest another girl was dead. And where in the meantime was he, this solid architect of the blameless life?

Well, there was one place where he and Moss had common ground. Green Acres.

Benson's young Mr Askew was courtesy itself to Mr Lennox. The respective solicitors had been in touch? Good, good. Askew rubbed his hands in expectation of a profitable commission, perhaps even promotion. Yes, of course Mr Lennox would wish to see the interior of the property. It was late afternoon but no matter, he would be pleased to show Mr Lennox round himself. Mrs Lennox? Kemp waved a deprecating hand. In Scotland for the shooting? Kemp could spin a tale with the best of them, and act a part when he had a mind to. He played the keen Mr Askew like a fish on a hook, and in no time the pair of them were humming their way through the autumn forest with the keys of Green Acres.

The trees were shedding early this year, robbed of sap by the long hot summer, and even the lawns around the house were into the sere and yellow blight.

Kemp found himself enjoying a feeling almost of belonging as they swept up the drive, and the young agent brought the car round in a final competent circle and parked at the porch door. This time the hornbeams are grinning at me, he thought, as I enter as of right. He followed Mr Askew into the wide hall and gazed about him.

Empty houses, he had found in his experience, hold little of their previous owners—there are few ghosts in modern rooms, in fitted wardrobes bare of clothes, pine bookshelves bereft of the books that furnished them, cold kitchens chastely screened, all living put away; thick carpets hold no footprints, and pale magnolia walls no evidence of personal taste—nor rancour either. All is as it should be: the occupants have departed, hail to those who come. If there had been violence in these felicitous environs, all had been swept under and into the perfect flooring, the insulated walls, and the double-glazing which now gave back no emanations of past words or deeds but simply existed in their own right, functionally perfect and above reproach.

Not that Kemp had expected to find any tangible echoes of the Pearsons in this house, handed over to them by Malcolm Moss for a mere song. Kemp thought of Moss's cold grey eyes and didn't believe a word of it. He looked around at the opulence—for opulence there was a-plenty. But no character apart from the design of the house itself which deserved better. Like the setting of that emerald ring... The interior of this home of the Pearsons had been bought off the peg, an expensive peg no doubt but one that catered for the ephemeral, luxury camping-out, the habitat of dwarfs.

He went back for another look at the kitchen, for there, despite the closed cupboards and silent machines, he had got the smell of something. Coffee, he wondered? A warmish odour, a latent aroma as of something cooked. He raised his nose like a Bisto kid, ignoring for the moment the screwball intensity of this young companion, hell-bent on the sale of the century. Kemp ran his hand over the top of the solid-fuel cooker, and carefully lifted the lid. Mr Askew was out on the porch by now, extolling the virtues of the patio. Kemp poked into the hole where kindling had been laid and drew out a charred scrap, a tiny piece of red white and blue border which crumbled in his fingers. So that was where Pearson's letter had gone.

He strolled outside, and said he might as well have a look at the garage. Mr Askew complied with enthusiasm. 'Very large double garage,' he said, walking across to it, 'and a stable—I understand the former owners kept a horse.'

The afternoon was collapsing into amorphous blue haze as they crossed the gravel drive. Mr Askew shook out the keys with a professional flourish, selected the right one and found the lock. The doors swung open to reveal the interior of a large handsome garage, and the rear of a white Rover.

Kemp felt no surprise, he merely turned to Askew with eyebrows raised in puzzled inquiry.

'What the devil...!' The young man was at a loss for words. He looked at the vehicle with shocked distaste as if it were an unlawful tenant. Which perhaps it was.

'Perhaps left by the previous owner?' Kemp remarked.

Askew was visibly affronted, but he gathered his resources manfully. 'Not at all. Quite impossible. Mr Pearson sold his car—I know that for a fact. It was a red Morgan.'

'You knew it?'

'Well, it happens I was interested. It was a great car, but—' Askew shrugged—'well, I actually couldn't afford it. Someone around here did buy it—I've seen it in Leatown since. But that isn't the point, Mr Lennox, this vehicle should not be here. Who on earth can it belong to?'

Kemp saw no reason to tell him. Instead he continued to act like a would-be purchaser only mildly diverted by the discovery of cockroaches in the basement.

'Never mind, Mr Askew, there's probably some good reason. Don't worry, I'm not expecting the car to be included with the fixtures and fittings. Now, can I see the rest of the outbuildings? I believe there's a stable?'

'Yes, yes, of course.' Mr Askew remembered his training: never let the sale situation get out of hand.

With a last perplexed glance at the white car, he left the garage doors swinging and led the way down the side of the paddock fence towards a lean-to building silhouetted against the dying glow of the western sky. Kemp followed him, their footsteps swishing through the long dried grasses with a sound like Time scything the harvest. The image came and went in Kemp's mind, but his apprehension remained as they reached the stable.

'This place doesn't lock,' said young Askew, pulling the bar out of the door, 'and there'll just be enough light to see.'

There was indeed. The square window high in the rafters still held sufficient of the sky to illuminate the scene below as if it were a stage set, as explicit in its drama as the pictured death of Chatterton.

On a bale of straw Malcolm Moss lay supine, one long arm trailing on the floor, and just beyond the limp fingers an upturned whisky bottle had spilled its contents, staining the dusty boards.

That much Kemp saw as he pushed Askew to one side and ran forward. He leant over Moss, lifted one of the closed eyelids and placed a knuckle lightly against the line of the jaw. He waited until he felt a faint irregular throb.

'He's alive,' he shouted back at Askew who was standing in the doorway twisting the bunch of keys in trembling hands, his eyes popping, his mouth half-open. 'Know anything about first aid?'

'Not much.' The young agent came stumbling over, 'I did a course once...'

'Well, now's your chance to practise it. Come on, let's get cracking.'

Malcolm Moss's face was ashen save for a blue line around his lips which were crusted with vomit, but as Kemp thrust probing fingers into the mouth and throat to clear the gullet he felt a shiver of breath across his hand. Askew spread his palms across the unconscious man's chest and for some minutes they worked in silence. At last Kemp took his own mouth away, and drew in a long breath.

'There's a pulse,' he said, panting. 'Go for a phone and get an ambulance. I suppose the phone's off at Green Acres?'

Askew nodded.

'I'll take my car,' he said tersely, 'there's a box at the crossroads. Who the hell is he? He doesn't look like a tramp.'

'It doesn't matter who he is. Get the ambulance. We've done all we can.'

When Askew had gone, Kemp prowled round the stable. On the far side of the bale he found a tumbler where it had rolled into a corner, and beside it an empty tablets bottle. It was too dark to read the chemist's label. Kemp looked carefully at the rest of the building. Along the far wall there ran a long bench where something white glimmered. He picked up the sheet of paper, and the fallen ballpoint, and went outside. In the fading light he could just make out the words:

My very dearest Frances—I can't go on. It's all going to have to come out and I cannot stand seeing you hurt. I hoped you would never have to know. Forgive me, but there's no other way. I love you—Malcolm

The last words were faint, and slid down the paper like the writing of a child.

Kemp put the note in his pocket. After all, he had a client and whether Malcolm Moss lived or died, these few lines belonged to her.

There was nothing more he could do for her husband. At least he was breathing. Kemp looked out wearily into the darkening trees, and was alarmed to feel a stab of disappointment. To end like this. He had taken Moss for a better man, a braver adversary, even if he were a killer. Or was it that he himself simply felt personally cheated because his quarry had escaped, and might yet, having gone the coward's way, also evade justice?

At last he heard the noise of the motor, and saw the headlights of the ambulance flashing through the trunks of the hornbeams.

No TIME WAS LOST in getting the unconscious man to Epping General Hospital. Kemp and Askew followed in Askew's car. The whizzkid was by now exhilarated by his part in the rescue, quite chuffed in fact by the ambulancemen's praise, which Kemp stood aside from and let him enjoy. It was Askew who answered the questions as to their patient's identity. 'There'll be something in his pockets... Oh, and there's a car in the garage...'

Kemp said nothing. He'd let them find out for themselves. All he did was hand over the empty chemist's bottle. 'The doctor'll want to know what he took besides the whisky.'

The man had grunted: 'Sleeping tablets... Why will they do it?' He'd seen it all before.

Kemp also let Askew deal with the inquiries at Reception once Moss had been taken into casualty. Askew was custodian of the property upon which this unhappy occurrence had intruded. Askew coped very well. He had found the registration documents in the Rover, they tied in nicely with the papers in the victim's pocket wallet—identity was established without a word from Kemp, who watched the proceedings like an uninvolved bystander at a street accident. He did note, however, that the name Malcolm Moss appeared to mean nothing to Askew.

They had a word with the doctor. 'Will he live?' asked Kemp with just the right modicum of interest.

'Too early to say. He meant to do it all right—massive dose, washed down with whisky. It was lucky for him that he was sick. But he wasn't in good shape before he took those pills, I reckon. We just don't know whether he'll pull through—too early to say. At least we know who he is—the police will contact his relatives.'

There seemed no point in their staying any longer. Kemp yawned.

'Well, Mr Askew it's time I was home. My car's still at your office.'

The young man suddenly realized he yet had a prospective client, and was full of apologies both fervent and inappropriate.

'Of course, Mr Lennox, I'd quite forgotten... We'd better get back there. All this... Terrible event... I can't say how sorry I am...'

Kemp appreciated his feelings; this was worse than finding the vendor had removed the staircase.

'It's not your fault,' he said magnanimously, 'but I shall have to phone my housekeeper—she must be wondering why I haven't been in for dinner.'

He closed the booth door firmly and dialled 72 Crownberry Avenue. This time, Frances Jessica was at home.

'Don't ask any questions. The police will come. Keep my name out of it.' He told her Malcolm had been found, he was unconscious but alive in Epping Hospital. He told her nothing else. 'Be surprised when they contact you. You have not heard the news from anyone else. Understand?'

She was quick. Even at a distance he could feel their thoughts running together. He put down the phone.

FOURTEEN

THAT NIGHT KEMP slept badly. It was not that he ever expected life to be a tidy packet nor for his cases to come out gift-wrapped and labelled, but he did prefer to see the pattern in the knitting. The only pattern he could discern in the Moss affair was one of loosely woven death. There had been two of them to date, all neatly explained as suicide and misadventure; and now another suicide which might, or might not, shed light on the others.

There were some mornings when he woke with his mind singing clear; this was not one of them. Brewing tea in a foul temper, he heard the rasp of his phone—always a harsher sound on such mornings when the nerves are particularly sensitive.

It was an excited McCready, a jubilant McCready.

'Get in here fast, laddie... We've cracked the Pearsons! I'll not tell you on the phone...'

'Why the hell not?' Kemp barked. 'Don't tell me they worked for the CIA. I couldn't bear it...' But the line went dead. McCready must be very pleased with himself, hugging his story like a teddy-bear, or else his Scottish instincts were on the alert for telephone bill economies. He was always having these sudden spurts of thrift. Kemp suspected Mrs McCready, for he knew they both spent happy evenings going over the Agency 'buiks' and it was ever her whine that office expenses would lead to eventual ruin.

This thought was still in his mind when he reached the office, so that he took the telex message from McCready's hand and grimaced at its length. Perhaps indeed his next month's salary was in jeopardy.

But McCready's face bore no evidence of reproach.

'Read that, Lennox.' McCready was striding up and down, barely concealing his excitement. But even when Kemp had come to the end of the American Agency report he was still mystified. There seemed nothing in it to warrant his employer's behaviour.

Leopold Pearson and his sister, Lucille, were both American citizens, although their mother, Leonie Ambrose, had been English. She had brought them to New York in 1938 when Leopold was five and Lucille under a year old. Leonie Ambrose had been a widow when she arrived in New York, she was apparently wealthy and when she married Culver Pearson she had married into more wealth. Both she and Culver were dead, having left a considerable fortune to Leopold and Lucille. They had lived high, there were apartments in New York, and a house in Westchester, but the money had been running out, and when they left for England last year creditors were pressing. Leopold had had several brushes with the law in the States on charges of fraud, his business dealings were shady, he was under investigation for tax evasion; so far as he could be traced he was now apparently in South America. Lucille had been wild and extravagant, and in and out of private mental homes for some years.

That was the gist of it. Kemp turned to McCready. 'So what?'

'Leonie Ambrose!' McCready all but exploded. 'You mean you've never heard of her?''

'Not until now. Who was she?'

'Just about the crookedest bitch that ever slipped through our fingers. You'll have heard of Lawrence Ambrose?'

Something stirred at the back of Kemp's memory, and the wires twanged along the circuits of his mind until they struck a spark.

'You mean the man who shot the policeman? What was his name, Cogan?'

'You've got it. The murderer of Jimmy Cogan. His name was Lawrence Ambrose. Aye, and they caught him, thank God, and he was hanged for it.'

'That was back in—nineteen-thirty-eight, wasn't it?'

The case had not merited any place in criminal law textbooks being devoid of dispute or any contentious legal point, but it had been a sensational event for all that, the shooting of a young constable on duty in circumstances both callous and cold-blooded.

'And Leonie Ambrose?'

'She was his wife, and she got away with the loot. Oh, we recovered some of it but she got most of the haul. Remember it now? Lawrence Ambrose was a high-class villain. He'd done time but he always managed to stash his ill-gotten gains. Then he did the big one—Hatton Garden firm just before Christmas nineteen-thirty-seven—he got the lot, jewellery, stones worth thousands, the whole caboosh.'

'But he didn't get away?'

McCready's eyes were bitter.

'Oh aye, he was caught. But not before he'd shot puir young Cogan. The lad hadn't long joined the Force when it happened. He was barely twenty-two. He was on patrol that night in Hatton Garden. Saw something suspicious and went to investigate, and got shot in the belly for his pains... He lived just long enough to give a description of the man who shot him. We picked Ambrose up, and he never denied the shooting, but the stuff was gone—and so had his wife...'

'How'd she manage it?'

McCready looked bleakly back over the changing years.

'Well, we'd got our man... Remember, Lennox, the murder of a policeman was what mattered then. The firm who were robbed—they'd get their insurance moneys—all we really cared about was Ambrose...'

McCready gave Kemp a sharp glance. 'And don't you give me any of your liberal ideas—this was the cold-blooded killing of a young policeman, and this was the Thirties. The public got what they wanted, and what they wanted was revenge. Oh aye, investigations were made, the police tried to keep track of people, the

fences, the jewel experts—but they found nothing...'

'And Leonie Ambrose got away with it?'

'She sailed from Liverpool even before her husband was hanged, taking her two children with her—
and a fine pair they've turned out. As well they might.
Rogue's blood is bad blood, always was...' It was a
favourite theme of McCready's: criminal families bred
criminals, he'd seen it happen over and over again
with a fine inevitability, at least in his own mind, that
that was how it would always be.

'And—' McCready was now jabbing a finger in
Kemp's face—'you can't blame that on a deprived
childhood. You've seen the report—the Pearsons were
rich, they had everything America had to offer to the
rich—good schools, colleges, all the contacts that
wealth brings. And just look where they end up. The
boy another crook like his father, and the girl by all
accounts a raving lunatic. Bad blood, Lennox, inherited bad blood...'

As McCready was obviously off on one of his phil-
osophic frolics, Kemp studied his blotter and said
nothing. Only when the diatribe was finished did he
give McCready an edited version of what had been
found at Green Acres the evening before.

McCready rubbed the end of his small pointed nose
and looked sagacious and disapproving at the same
time.

'I don't see why you should go rooting about out
there. Suicide, eh? Well, that never solved anything.

But if you're right and he killed the Pearson girl—well, that might give you an answer. Most suicides leave a note, was there one?'

Kemp gave scarcely a second's thought to the niceties of truth, and shook his head. Frances Jessica was still his client and he owed her his discretion; the paper found beside her husband belonged to her.

'Those two, the Pearsons—they were a right bad lot,' went on McCready. 'Could be they tried to con your Malcolm Moss. Perhaps they were playing that—what-do-you-call-it?—badger game...' McCready wasn't too sure of his animals in the jungle of American crime. 'Mebbe Lucille was the bait and Moss fell for it. Then Moss finds out and kills her, and he and the brother have to cover up. Exit Leopold to South America so that no more questions are asked. I dunno, Lennox... On the other hand, this report shows Lucille's been round the twist for years—she could still have drowned herself.'

Kemp let him prattle on. There were already far too many plausible explanations just as there were still too many loose ends sticking out. He told McCready about the death of Angela Foster.

'Have a word with your chum Comfrey, will you? Otherwise that inquest also will be over, and everyone satisfied it was an accident.'

'H'm.' McCready scratched his nose again. 'I'll see what I can do. But if Moss was up there in his car that night, who's to prove he knocked her off her bike? And why should he do it, anyway?'

Kemp was also trying to work that one out.

'She was never asked at the inquest whether any-one else was staying with the Pearsons. Perhaps she saw Moss there. Perhaps he thought she'd eventually talk about it, and he'd get involved... It would be easy enough to run her down if he saw her leaving The Oak.'

'You think she might have threatened him? Is that what took him back to Green Acres?'

Kemp shrugged.

'I think he still had keys to the place—easy enough for him, he was the architect.'

McCready snorted.

'You'd never prove it wasn't an accident. And don't you go interfering with inquests—coroners are touchy people, think of your own reputation.'

'I haven't got one, and well you know it.' The feel-ing of working always in the dark like a mole was be-ginning to annoy Kemp. People kept throwing explanations at him as if he were of weak intellect. He didn't like it, no more than he liked the idea that An-gela Foster might have threatened Moss. All that wild talk of hers about the tall man and the green stones. He hadn't told McCready about that, nor about the stone in the scarf. He'd given a half-promise to Ja-mie. If young Angie had really nicked it from her mistress it wouldn't do the Foster family any good for that fact to be introduced into the inquest. Nor would they welcome any delay in getting the tragedy over and done with and their poor lass buried; there were other reputations at stake besides Kemp's, and the dead have no right of reply.

'Leave it alone, man,' McCready interrupted his thoughts abruptly. Kemp marked the change in address; he was 'laddie' when being given friendly advice, he grew to adult status when it came to taking orders. He resented this also.

'It's my holiday,' he said defensively. 'Besides, I still have a client.'

'Yon woman! She's led you a fair dance, her and that husband of hers. Well, if he lives, mebbe you'll get at the truth.'

Kemp doubted it, but once McCready had stumped out of the room he phoned the hospital.

Not being a relative, he was given short shrift and no information but on crisply informing the receptionist that as it was he, Mr Lennox, who might have saved the patient's life and he was anxious to ascertain whether that life was still in being, he was told to wait. A warmer voice told him that Mr Moss was still unconscious but holding on. Kemp asked if Mrs Moss was there.

'She's at her husband's bedside. Would you like to speak to her?'

Frances Jessica's voice was thin and far away.

'You saved him.'

'I hope so.'

'He's very ill. They're not sure yet if he will recover.'

'I'm sorry. I have something for you. I've not shown it to anyone. I took it from the place where he was found. He must have written it just before he became unconscious.'

There was a long silence.

'Are you there, Mrs Moss?'

'Yes, I'm here. Will you read it to me?'

Kemp spread the piece of paper on his blotter and without expression read the words out to her.

Again there was a long pause. Kemp began to wonder if he was doing the right thing.

'Are you sure those are the exact words?'

'I am reading you what he wrote, Mrs Moss,' Kemp said patiently. 'Look, don't worry about it now, but I want to know when Malcolm is able to talk. I'll give you my private number where you can reach me.' He suddenly remembered the Plenders' dinner party. 'As a matter of fact I shall be out at Leatown this evening—there's another number you can call me at there...'

Her soft voice gave him thanks, no more, and it was she who finally rang off.

KEMP SPENT THAT Friday afternoon at various newspaper offices scanning their files of the late Thirties. The journalism of that time differed from its counterpart in the Sixties. It seemed not to have been considered so necessary then for the populace to be fed on the pabulum of scurrilous detail now judged essential to their diet. The chicken was served up, so to speak, without the spicy stuffing. Somehow it made the bare facts more horrendous. In the Ambrose case the public had assuredly howled for vengeance and been given it in full measure. There were allowed to be no mitigating circumstance. An eye for an eye, a tooth for a tooth, a life for a life; it was simple justice and seen to be so. Only the small band of protestants against capital punishment outside the gaol that bleak morning struck an incongruent note—like a bunch of CND supporters at a nuclear missile base.

By the time the last grim scene had been enacted Leonie Ambrose and her two children had left the port of Liverpool for the New World—as one reporter had somewhat extravagantly put it—'like early settlers fleeing from a tormented Europe'. But Leonie had been no refugee, of that Kemp was certain, except in the sense that she was escaping the attention of the Press. They had got as much mileage out of her as they could. There had been not only the combination of pathos and dreadful fulfilling of justice in the drama of the execution itself, but the stolen jewels captured the imagination of the reporters as well as the public. Rewards had been offered, all possible leads to their recovery were investigated, but no one had come forward with information, and eventually it was assumed that they had disappeared into the trough of the criminal underworld where mouths were kept tightly shut; even the small fry at these depths were not talking. No one wanted to be in any way implicated or associated now with the man who had killed a policeman in cold blood.

It was a long task for Lennox Kemp pursuing Leonie Ambrose through the interstices of bygone newspaper history, but one very much to his taste for he had the proper innate curiosity of the born archivist. What is written in the past, the things said and reported, no matter how inaccurately (the very inaccuracies and distortions being themselves the trimmings of the story), are the very stuff of research, fascinating to seekers after truth, ever hopeful of discovering some titbit to reinforce a theory, make good a hypothesis.

So he continued to look everywhere for some small fact, some inkling of a hint that would link up with the half-formed shapes flitting through his mind like hordes of blind bats clawing the night caves for foothold.

FIFTEEN

DRIVING OUT TO LEATOWN, he still had the Ambrose case on his mind, but as he crossed the marshes where the grey dinosaur outlines of the mechanical diggers crouched round their water-holes in the gravel pits, he shook his mind free and contemplated the evening ahead.

In the district the burden of the past lay heavily upon his personal life, stretching unwelcome tentacles into the present. A remark made by Frances Jessica came into his mind, reviving the peace of that sunny afternoon at Crownberry Avenue and bringing with it another kind of nostalgia, this time a yearning for some unattainable paradise. What was it she had said? 'If it had been by Ibsen, he'd have begun it fifteen years later...' They had been discussing literary loves and hates. There was something else she had said—was it when they were talking about Flaubert? A chance observation, it hovered now on the edges of his mind.

As he turned in at the Plenders' drive the sharp tooth of memory bit momentarily on an old sore. So many evenings Muriel and he had been there; for drinks, for bridge, for companionship in the easy way of friendship, for the spurious security of belonging, as they had done then, to a set... He was relieved to find it really didn't matter any more.

Robin greeted him at the door in quite the old style, exuding bonhomie, instantly reassuring.

'Hullo there, Lennox. We're so pleased to see you. Betty and I got talking, you know, after I saw you that day in Leatown, and we thought, well, there's no reason why we shouldn't get together again...'

Betty, in ankle-length chiffon, gave Kemp a soft handshake. No kiss yet, though it had been the custom in the past. Kemp wondered what they required of him to regain that state of grace.

The Plenders' house was old and capacious, having been built for a dual purpose, part doctor's family residence, part surgery and dispensary. Betty's elegant modernizing hand could be detected in the furnishings but Robin's inertia had prevented too much depredation of original features, so that the house retained its charm harmoniously enough with the up-to-date comfort of central heating and insulation.

On his way through to the drawing-room Kemp said he'd have a word with Rose, Betty's maid and personal treasure.

'Go ahead,' said Robin, 'you'll find her in the kitchen.'

Kemp glanced into the working centre of the house, a high-ceilinged room where an awesome array of iron bells still hung above the door leading to the stone-flagged passage and the old dispensary. Rose turned from the dials of the modern cooker which had displaced the ancient stove, and gave Kemp the warmest smile of welcome he had received since his return to Leatown. He had always liked Rose. Somewhere back in time she had got into trouble and the trouble had been fostered in outer Essex where by now it must have grown up enough to have troubles of its own. The Plenders had given Rose work and a home. And it was a good home, for although Robin and Betty were not always kindly people, having their full share of superficial foibles, they wished to be seen as such. In return Rose gave them loyalty and absolute discretion; nothing heard in that house by Rose would ever be aired beyond its doors.

Kemp said to her now: 'A call may come for me tonight. It'll be from a woman. Could you slip me the word—carefully?'

Rose gave him a knowing look, and nodded.

'You can take it down in the dispensary, Mr Kemp, there's still a phone there.'

The other dinner guests, a Mr and Mrs Latham—the names meaning as little to Kemp as their faces which were in no way memorable—were already well into a second round of drinks when Kemp joined them, but he sensed an atmosphere of expectation in the room. The lion of this particular dinner party had apparently not so far arrived.

Robin came over with a drink and confided: 'We've asked the Sefts tonight to meet you. Thought it a good idea that you and he should get to know each other better after that rather unfortunate start.'

So that was it. Kemp wondered why on earth it should matter so much to Robin Plender until he remembered Tony Egerton's words: '... married to the daughter of Sir Herbert Smithers...' The medical profession also had its own small snobberies.

Another round of drinks and trivial conversation had passed, and Kemp noticed that Betty was becoming anxious and watching the clock, when there was the roar of a car engine outside, the squeal of tyres and the banging of doors. Kemp recognized the sound, and casually moved the curtains at the window. So, it was everybody's favourite doctor, the new partner, who had acquired Leopold Pearson's car. The question was, when?

He stood back by the fireplace so that he could take a fairly distanced view of Benjamin Seft.

Kemp had to admit that, groomed for the evening and without the untidy appearance he had had in the surgery, Seft had great presence. He was possibly not so young as he looked, nearer forty than thirty, but he was certainly very large and possessed of a dynamic quality. He gave the impression of being a man who demanded, and by his demeanour was in the habit of getting, immediate attention. He had entered the room ahead of his wife—no nonsense about ladies first— and going over to Betty he clasped her to him and kissed her warmly, presumably in apology for being late.

He shook Kemp's hand with a fierce grip. 'No hard feelings? Had a bad surgery that day, I'm afraid.'

Seft's good looks were of the craggy type supposed to be irresistible to women, and he had wolfish good teeth to match. So had little Red Riding Hood's grandmother, thought Kemp irrelevantly, smarting from the handshake. It had been strong enough to crush his fingers and fervent enough to endanger his glass of sherry, so he put it down carefully on the mantelshelf. In doing so he missed the entrance of Mrs Seft.

Robin brought her over to him, and Kemp was suddenly faced with both the Sefts together which, for one of his small stature, was quite an experience. For she too was tall, in height almost equal to her husband.

Her husky voice said 'Hello' as she looked down at him, but Kemp could have sworn that she hardly saw him for her dark eyes were full of ill-concealed anger and her not unhandsome features were set and hard as an African carving—which indeed they resembled.

It was a reasonably warm night and the Plenders' house was always too hot, but Mrs Seft—Judith as she had been introduced to Kemp—refused to be parted from the mandarin-style jacket buttoned up to her throat over her long bright green crêpe dress.

Well, perhaps she was annoyed with her husband for keeping them late, perhaps they had had a row in the car driving over, whatever it was Ben Seft had shaken it off while she continued to seethe, nursing her wrath to keep it warm. Kemp recognized the familiar signals even as he murmured the commonplace banalities suitable for the occasion. That marriage can be a battle-ground was no news to him. The protagonists sometimes prefer a wider audience, and a social evening out can give the opportunity for widening the conflict, adding zest and bite to positions already dug in on the domestic front. He sensed the omens in the air-space between the Sefts, and while reflecting that it boded ill for the success of the dinner party, he could not help but feel a certain sardonic amusement.

Judith Seft accepted a large martini from her host and spilled some as she sat down beside Lillian Latham. Her hand was shaking. Kemp wondered if she had been drinking before she came. Since their arrival neither husband or wife had looked at one another; they were like opposing generals who had drawn up their plans of action, taken their battle stations and knew that a word, a glance might give away their strategy to the enemy.

Kemp sipped his sherry. Lennox, he said to himself, you're getting fanciful again.

As there was feminine talk at the sofa end the men drew together in a group by the fireplace. Seft had been to an exhibition of medical equipment and was full of his own enthusiasm; he had the air of being an exceptional man which set the rest of them at a premium. He rather adroitly brought Kemp within the sphere of the discussion, hinting to Latham—that Kemp was in business, without stating what precise position he occupied in the commercial world—a manoeuvre which Kemp appreciated as not being without wit.

To further that line of business, and to get his own back for the handshake, Kemp remarked casually: 'I gather you've got another inquest coming up in a day or two...' It was a perfectly natural comment to make in the presence of local doctors, particularly when one of them was the police surgeon. 'I think I knew the unfortunate girl—Angela Foster, wasn't it?'

Robin Plender merely said, 'Rotten thing to happen. That family's had their full share of trouble.'

'As a matter of fact it was I who found her,' said Seft in an easy tone. 'Poor kid, she came quite a cropper on that road.'

'Was she concussed when you got to her?' asked Kemp.

Seft looked at him as if he'd said a bad word. 'She'd a fractured skull,' he said with the brutal realism of the professional who knows his stuff, and added, for the benefit of the layman who had put such an impertinent query, 'You don't talk about concussion when there's fatal injury. Simple fact, Mr Kemp—if I hadn't found her she'd have died where she lay.'

The ladies, overhearing, shivered among themselves. It was not the kind of subject they tolerated even at medical dinner parties. Bone and flesh might be the concern of their husbands but to talk of it outside hours was tantamount to rudeness, excluding as it did their own interests which tended more to gossip. In exercise of this function the little Latham woman tried to widen the issue, away from the nastier aspects of medical detail.

'Didn't she work for those Pearson people up the hill?'

The name was as welcome as a shark in the swimming pool. It jolted Judith's drinking elbow so that half the contents of her glass splashed down the front of her embroidered jacket. There was commiseration and much dabbing with handkerchiefs, and in the middle of the small turmoil Rose announced dinner.

Kemp was the last to take his seat in the panelled dining-room and he saw that Judith Seft was at last being persuaded to relinquish her jacket which was whisked smartly away by Rose who said she would expunge the offending drops. Judith sat opposite Kemp with Ben further up the table on her side, on the right hand of the hostess with whom he was deeply engaged in conversation so that he could not directly see his wife even had he wanted to, which did not appear to be the case.

As he spooned his soup Kemp glanced across at Judith. The signs of repressed anger were gone but there was still a tenseness about her, and in some obscure way, a defiant nervousness. With her dark chestnut hair coiled and piled on top of her head she seemed taller than ever, an effect further accentuated by her long swan-like neck. Kemp was reminded of Tenniel's Alice swaying like a serpent above the tree-tops. Round this graceful white pillar was wreathed a heavy twisted chain bearing pendent-fashion five great green stones set in silver. They caught and held the lamplight, breaking it up on the facets in glittering pinpoints of flame as the necklace swung against her throat.

Kemp was conscious of staring as her eyes met his but hers flickered away as, under lowered lids, she looked along the table in the direction of her husband.

Once again it was Lillian Latham who quite unconsciously set the ball rolling.

'Judith,' she said, leaning across the table, 'don't think me rude but that is the most beautiful necklace.'

Everyone stopped talking and looked at it. But Kemp looked at Benjamin Seft. The doctor's face went white and the blue enamel eyes hardened. He pushed his chair back as if to rise but thought better of it, and took himself under control. To Kemp, watching him intently, it was as if a surge of sea was halted and contained by a breakwater. But the effort showed in the tightness around Seft's mouth, and as he threw down his napkin on the table it was creased as though by an iron where it had been gripped.

Judith had put up a trembling hand, and was fingering the twisted chain. 'Yes,' she drawled but with a touch of bravado, 'don't the green stones perfectly match my dress?'

'I've never seen you wear it before, Judith,' said Betty. 'Is it a recent acquisition?'

'As a matter of fact,' said Judith, 'I found it—and if you want to know where—under a gooseberry bush.'

Everyone laughed, thankful to have the tension relieved, except Ben Seft who was staring straight ahead with all the concentration of someone about to be asked a test question.

Kemp felt it was time for him to throw in his little twopennyworth.

'Quite a find, Mrs Seft,' he said, 'they really are magnificent emeralds. Their setting, if you'll forgive me saying so, is perhaps not worthy of their true value.'

'Come on, Judith,' said Betty, 'tell us . . . I'm sure they were a present from Ben.'

Pleased now with the effect she had had on her husband, which may well have been her aim, Judith's tone lightened.

'Of course they were,' she said with only barely discernible sarcasm. 'An unbirthday present. Isn't that so, Ben dear?'

Now that he had taken himself in hand, Ben dear turned towards her calmly.

'That's right, Judith. I just didn't expect you to find it so soon but as it goes with your dress tonight, I'll forgive your pre-emption. As a matter of fact,' he now addressed the whole table, 'the necklace was part of a legacy left me recently by an aunt. I intended to give it to Judith for her birthday but I see I have been forestalled. No matter . . . But isn't this all getting rather personal? Let's talk about something else.'

Robin poured more wine, and general chatter rose once more among the company. Kemp noticed that

Robin still dispensed wine in fairly large quantities in much the same manner as he over-prescribed placebos in his practice—and possibly on the same premise, which was that if a little of what you fancy does you good then you'll do a hell of a lot better on more. As he took yet another bottle from the sideboard it struck Kemp that everybody was drinking a good deal. Kemp covered his own glass, and resolved to be careful. He knew that there often comes a moment at dinner parties such as this, where there has already been a scene of some tension, when everyone unbuttons, voices grow higher, atmosphere intensifies and an air of hidden drama gives even the salt-cellars and spoons an amplified significance. Such a moment seemed to have arrived.

An argument had developed between Latham and Seft on the subject of state aid to industry. Kemp found it rather boring but he shot his ears forward when Ben Seft suddenly rounded on Robin.

'It's just like that bloody scheme for trainee doctors. Paying old GPs who'd already made their pile out of private practice to take on impecunious medicos. Working the poor chaps to the bone, then booting them out before offering them any future in the practice, and getting in another subsidized lot!'

Robin, who had been sharing with Kemp some quiet reminiscences about old Leatown characters they had both known, looked up startled by what seemed to be an attack.

'Oh, come off it, Ben,' he exclaimed, 'that's not fair—you got your partnership all right. I know the scheme used to be abused at first but that's all over and done with long ago.'

Before he could continue, Judith Seft, whose glass had been filled and emptied rather more than the others, took her chance to re-open the marital skirmish.

'Since when were you an impecunious medico?' she inquired, scathingly, leaning forward to glare at her husband so that the emeralds swung and sparkled above her green dress. 'You never wanted for a penny after you married me!'

Kemp was aware of Lillian Latham's neat head wagging like a tennis spectator between the adversaries, avid for points. What a predatory little bird it is, he reflected, the suburban housewife scenting prey.

'That's got nothing to do with it,' muttered Seft, thrown off his argument by the intervention. 'I'm talking about professional skills being prostituted ...'

'My, my, what words we're using.' Judith contemplated the red depths of her glass. 'You're talking about money. You always do. You're obsessed with it.' She brought the glass up to her lips. 'And you never had any aunts who'd leave you so much as a string of beads!' she added viciously under her breath.

Fortunately Rose arrived with baked Alaska and pineapple kirsch, and the moment passed as such moments must, but Kemp observed that they were all caught up in a situation where each of them—with the possible exception of the Plenders—had an interest in sustaining the drama. The Lathams for a certainty would dine out on this night's scene for weeks to come, the Sefts had their own reasons for using the company as a sounding-board for their matrimonial in-fighting and as a means of airing resentments, and as for Kemp—well, he felt his job was his justification. So much of his work tended towards anti-climax. There would be peaks of high activity, then a drop to an arid plateau where nothing happened; the Moss case had been no exception, and indeed seemed to have come to an end with the attempted suicide. He had not expected that the Plender dinner party would throw him further bones to gnaw on.

Now he wanted very urgently to know why Judith Seft was wearing such amazing emeralds simply to spite her husband and why his reaction had been so powerful. The man himself intrigued Kemp; Seft positively fizzed with untapped energy, you expected it to come out of his ears in electric sparks.

As Betty Plender was serving the desserts, Rose came back into the room. She leaned over Kemp's chair and whispered to him.

'Excuse me,' Kemp said, rising and following her out.

'I've put the call through to the dispensary, Mr Kemp,' she said with a knowing look, 'you won't be disturbed in there.'

It took Kemp some time to switch on the lights down the passage, and find the telephone beside the sink in the tiled room where old Dr Plender used to patter about in his carpet slippers putting up Gregory's mixture in little packets. Kemp looked back before he closed the door but there was no one in the corridor.

He heard Frances Jessica's voice as he picked up the telephone. To his first inquiry she answered: 'No, Malcolm is just the same but the doctors say he's stronger. But there's something else... That note you read out to me. I simply couldn't bear to think about it straight away... They say he took an overdose of his sleeping pills. It's true he has been using sleeping tablets lately, and he did have a prescription to get some last Monday—the day he didn't come home. And the bottle was from our local chemist...'

Kemp waited as her voice shook but when she spoke again it was in a firmer tone.

'But, Lennox... Malcolm never called me Frances. I've always been Jessica to him, never anything else. Why would he, at a time like that, call me by a name I never use?'

Kemp put a hand to his forehead.

'You're sure that's what he wrote?' There was an urgent note now in her voice.

'I'm quite sure,' he answered.

'And they say he took some whisky. Malcolm never drank whisky. It made him sick. He never touched it. Yet they say there was a bottle of whisky near where he was found.'

Kemp's thoughts were racing.

'Don't say anything more now. Stay with him. Don't leave him. I'll bring you that note as soon as I can.'

As he put down the phone Kemp was certain he heard a click. Damn it, he thought, in a doctor's house there are many telephones. Passing through the kitchen he said to Rose, 'Sorry about that. I'd forgotten one shouldn't take up telephone time in a medical household.'

'That's all right, Mr Kemp. There's none of them on duty tonight. They've got the young assistant on this weekend.'

When Kemp returned to the dining-room the first thing he heard was Betty scolding the menfolk for holding up the pudding course. 'The ice-cream's all melted,' she wailed to no one in particular, but Kemp noticed that on Ben Seft's plate as on Robin's it was true. He himself had chosen pineapple so could not be blamed.

Both Betty and Robin continued to pour the civilizing lubricant of conversation upon the troubled waters. If the evening had not in fact procured the result they had hoped for—which Kemp surmised had been to show him that all was well within the partnership of Plender and Seft—they were still determined that all was not lost.

The talk had turned to families. The Lathams, it appeared, shared problems with the Plenders over their respective offspring, the upbringing, the training, and the ultimately discordant aims of the coming generation. Kemp could allow his thoughts to drift through this discussion, thankful that at least Muriel and he had not contributed to the world's troubles by having children. Neither it seemed had the Sefts, although this situation was obviously not accepted by Judith with any satisfaction.

'You're all lucky to have something...some stake in the future,' she remarked darkly to the table at large. 'What have we got?'

'Well, jewellery like that for one thing,' replied Lillian Latham somewhat tartly. 'David couldn't afford to buy me anything so beautiful, Judith.'

'And your husband doesn't spend his time chasing neurotic girls, I bet...' The amount of liquor Judith had consumed was beginning to show and her voice was slurred. Kemp could not tell who, apart from himself, heard her but he saw Robin give Betty a sharp look.

'Coffee in the other room,' she said, rising quickly, 'Come along, everyone—let Rose clear away.'

Benjamin Seft refused any liqueur, drank his coffee up quickly and looked at his watch. 'It's that Mrs Bate,' he said to Robin, 'there's a danger of pneumonia. I think I'd better look in on her.'

'Nonsense, old chap, young Abbott can handle it.'

'I'd much rather go myself.' Seft turned to Betty with what must often have been his winning smile, 'Sorry, my dear, to break up the party...'

'But I don't want to go home yet,' said Judith stubbornly, taking another drink from her hostess who exclaimed: 'Don't worry about Judith, Ben, we'll see she gets home all right.' Seft looked nonplussed but the Lathams broke in together volunteering to take Judith in their car, it was on their way, they would be only too happy.

Judith was more relaxed now, bent on enjoying the rest of the evening, flaunting her emeralds as if, having passed the Rubicon, she cared not as to the outcome.

'I hate driving in that bloody red monster of his, anyway,' she said, 'I wanted to come in the saloon tonight, but he insisted on his own car. It musses up my hair, and he knows it . . .'

Kemp waited just long enough to hear the roar of the engine die away before he took Robin aside.

'I'm sorry to be a nuisance but I'd appreciate it if I could use your phone again . . .'

'Sure, use the one in the study. You know where it is.'

It was a rare occurrence for McCready to be disturbed in the sanctity of his own home, particularly at such a late hour for he and Mrs McCready went early to bed, but Kemp was impelled by a strong sense that for somebody time was running out.

Talking his way through the protestations of the awakened Scot standing pyjama-clad and bare of foot at the other end of the phone, Kemp patiently explained over and over again precisely what it was he wanted. The expostulations came thick and fast as McCready took in the enormity of the request.

'You're mad, Lennox... I can't do that!'

'I have to get to Comfrey through you. He'll not believe me.'

'And I canna believe you either... You've got a bee in your bonnet over this case...'

Kemp took it slowly from the beginning. At least McCready was listening now, and Kemp didn't care any more whether anyone else was.

'It's not a lot to ask,' he finished, tired out with the effort to think and talk persuasively at the same time. 'Comfrey or one of his men, that's all I ask...'

'Are you sure of your facts?'

'Pretty sure. There was another child. She didn't take him with them. He was older than the others— she likely thought he'd give the game away.'

'And you think...'

'There's no time for all that now. Get Comfrey on the phone before it's too late.'

Kemp sat back in Robin's armchair and looked at the study clock. It was forty minutes' drive to Epping; perhaps it was already too late.

He lifted the phone again and dialled the hospital. He knew it would do no good trying to talk to the medical staff—they wouldn't listen to him. But perhaps she would.

She did. She never ceased to surprise him. She who accepted everything as it came.

SIXTEEN

DESPITE JUDITH'S INSISTENCE that the party must go on there was a chilly unease about the scene in the Plenders' sitting-room when Kemp returned to it, and within a short time the Lathams were exclaiming they had not realized the lateness of the hour. It did not prove difficult for Kemp to prise Judith away from any prior adherence to them. He had drunk a good deal less and was more on his toes so that when it came to leave-taking in the porch it was he who ushered the redoubtable Mrs Seft, emeralds and all, into his small car. As she folded herself up in the front seat and was silent, Robin gave directions to her home.

She was an attractive woman, Kemp decided, if you liked the fighting type; bedding her would be as tough as felling a giant tree—but the sweetness might well be intensified by the strength of the target brought low.

For most of the journey to the other side of Leatown where the land opened out towards the Essex countryside, she remained silent, wrapped in what could be post-alcoholic stupor, but she must eventually have felt that Lennox Kemp deserved something better than speechless solitude, or perhaps some residue of social nicety asserted itself for, as the cool night air revived her, she spoke:

'I'm sorry, Mr Kemp. I'm not usually like this. I'm afraid I've not been very sociable tonight but I had had a shock. There's no reason why I should take it out on you.'

She groped in her bag for cigarettes and lighter while Kemp gave her the benefit of the pause.

'I shouldn't have worn the necklace. It's true, though, that I did find it. Are you married, Mr Kemp?'

'I have been.'

'Then you'll know how married couples be-have...' She was speaking very clearly, the way peo-ple tend to do when they have been drinking and by excessive clarity of diction they wish to make plain things confused in their minds.

'Yesterday I mislaid my car keys. Ben was out and I was in a hurry. I knew he had a spare set some-where... I never go into the drawers of his dressing-room—Ben's very particular about such things. He won't even let the servants put away his laundry, in-sists on doing everything himself... Isn't that odd? Of course he never had any servants till he married me, and I'll bet he was a tidy little boy... Where was I? Oh yes, anyway, I was rooting about in one of the draw-ers and right at the back I found this rolled-up bag. It was an old thing, all dirty, but do you know what, Mr Kemp? It was stuffed with jewellery...'

'Real jewellery?'

'Oh yes. I'm not an expert but I know good from bad. Funny, though, you saying that about the settings. All the stones were real enough. There were a lot of loose ones, all cut but not set. And there were some rings and brooches and other pieces, though the settings looked a bit amateurish. But the stones were fabulous—especially the emeralds, that's why I took this one—they matched my dress. And tonight I thought, what the hell? Ben was being so beastly about his car... So I dashed upstairs just before we left and put the necklace on.'

'You didn't tell him what you'd found?'

'Why should I? He can have his secrets—he's always had them. His aunt indeed! That's rubbish. He's never had any relatives, he came from nowhere. He made his way by scholarships. He's clever, I'll grant him that... My father—you know that Sir Herbert Smithers is my father?—well, he helped Ben. Said he'd make a brilliant surgeon.' Judith gave a surprisingly girlish giggle, not without malice. 'Dad wasn't so pleased when I married his brightest pupil, though. No more money from there for young Benjamin, he had to depend on mine... And then the brilliant scholar failed as a surgeon—too rough with his hands, I guess... My God, you'd have thought the world had come to an end. All that ambition turned bitter. So here he is a suburban GP...' There was some satisfaction in her voice.

'It doesn't look a bad life to me,' observed Kemp mildly. 'And you still don't know anything about his early background? Doesn't he ever talk about where he was brought up?'

'Taboo subject. He must have sprung full-grown from the head of Zeus... He does tend to act a bit godlike. More likely he came from the backstreets of some provincial dump.' Judith spoke with all the complacency of a Londoner born and bred, and sure of her position.

She had lapsed once again into a morose silence by the time they drew up outside her house, which was in darkness, but she made no move to get out of the car.

Kemp switched off the engine and waited.

Suddenly she spoke. 'Would you do something for me, Mr Kemp?'

'Yes, if I can.'

'I'm really awfully worried about that jewellery I found,' she said, hesitantly but with determination. 'Would you mind coming in and looking at it? You could be a kind of... witness... that it really exists. Otherwise no one will believe me. Would you? Come on, then...'

Her mind made up, she was out of the car and unlatching the gate. Kemp followed her up the long drive which curved to the front of the house and disappeared into shrubberies at the rear.

'The servants are off for the weekend, and it doesn't look as if Ben's back yet.' She had her keys out and was unlocking the door. Kemp only hoped that she was right. Warily he looked about for the red car and would have liked to investigate the rest of the drive but it was screened by bushes, and anyway she was calling out to him, peremptory now.

When he got into the hall she had switched on the lights and, plucking up her long green skirt, she stumbled up the central staircase leading to a gallery.

He went up after her. She had thrown open one of the doors leading off the landing, and he heard her pulling out drawers.

'They've gone!'

He followed her voice, and found her standing beside a tallboy in what was obviously her husband's dressing-room. She was emptying out a medley of ties, handkerchiefs and boxes of cufflinks and flinging them wildly on the floor.

'They've gone,' she cried again. 'Now nobody will believe they were ever here!'

'I believe they were there.'

'Why are you so interested?' The effects of drink were wearing off and her voice was sharper.

Kemp shrugged. 'You asked me to come. But now I'm here I'll ask you something. Do you know a man called Malcolm Moss?'

'Never heard of him.' Kemp believed her. She was in no condition to dissemble.

'Or a girl called Lucille Pearson?'

Her eyes shifted. She began to pick up aimlessly the things she had scattered on the floor.

'Pearson? Wasn't that the name of those people out at High Beech? Didn't the girl commit suicide?' Judith didn't look at Kemp but the ties she was holding slid down from her fingers.

Kemp took her firmly by the shoulders and sat her down on a chair. Her eyes refused to meet his.

'You're not suggesting Ben had anything to do with her?' There was a harsh note in her attempt at a laugh. 'He doesn't have time to have affairs and anyway he hates neurotic women. You can forget Miss Lucille Pearson... My dear man, she was real walking-wounded, that one. Mad as a hatter...'

'Perhaps she ran after him,' Kemp put it casually. 'Neurotic women do have fixations sometimes on their doctors.'

She looked up at him then, eagerly grasping the straw held out to her.

'That's what Robin said. It wasn't Ben's fault. She was his patient—but she was really mental. Well, it came out at the inquest, didn't it?'

'And the practice would have suffered if it had also come out she was having an affair with your husband?'

Kemp couldn't keep some bitterness out of his voice; he had guessed the cause for closing the ranks of the medicals, but he knew it wasn't the whole story. Seft was a very persuasive talker, Robin Plender liked a quiet life and could easily be led back into it by any threat of scandal. But Kemp still remained sceptical about Benjamin Seft. Whatever his relationship with Lucille Pearson, he didn't look the type to risk his career for a mad girl. Nor did Malcolm Moss for that matter. Why did everyone seem to assume that Lucille was some kind of femme fatale—mad, bad, and dangerous to know?

Kemp decided he wasn't going to learn much more tonight from Judith Seft. She looked sick now, drained alike of anger and vitality. She slowly undid the top buttons of her restored jacket and the action reminded her of the necklace. She tore it from her neck and threw it at Kemp's feet. He obligingly stooped and picked it up. People kept giving him emeralds. He turned the stones between his fingers; they burned green, brilliant and hostile. Whatever their bloodstained past and whatever dirty hands had touched them, the gems themselves remained indifferent to human motive, and would outlast all cupidity.

'I really must be going, Judith,' he said. There seemed nothing further he could do in that house tonight.

But as he heard the soft footfall behind him, he knew he was wrong.

'I agree, Mr Kemp. It's high time you were on your way.' Benjamin Seft's voice was quiet, bland as buttermilk, just the kind to allay the fears of a nervous patient.

KEMP WONDERED just how long he had been standing outside the open door. With a squirrel's instinct Kemp let the necklace slide into his pocket but he knew that Seft had seen it. With a fixed smile almost of con-

tempt, the big doctor strode past him as Judith, revived by the appearance of her husband, rose to her
feet, her face stormy. The Sefts confronted one another. It looked like being a battle of the Titans and
Kemp half-hoped he might be allowed to sneak off,
but his curiosity got the better of his discretion.

He watched as Seft with deliberate yet restrained
ferocity clipped his wife smartly on the side of the
head, and she fell on the rug like a snapped stick of
rhubarb.

Seft turned to Kemp.

'Sorry I had to do that. She's troublesome when
she's had too much to drink. Help me put her into
bed. Take her feet, will you, Mr Kemp, and let's make
her comfortable.'

Kemp admired the man's nerve. Seft certainly had
a way with him and expected others to go along with
it. He found himself cradling Judith's patent leather
shoes against his chest with one hand while support-
ing her elegant legs with the other as he and Seft carried her into the adjoining room and placed her on the
bed. Seft switched on the bedside lamp. He was still
wearing his scarf and gloves. During the transport of
Judith, Kemp's mind had been struggling with the
time element: Seft had left the Plenders an hour and
ten minutes ago; even in the red car it was at least forty
minutes' drive to Epping Hospital; there hadn't been
time. Seft had come for the jewels first, which was an
interesting priority.

Seft now bent over his wife, removed her shoes carefully with his gloved hands, placed one beside the bed and laid the other upturned by the door. Then without noticeable haste he took Kemp's arm in a firm grip and under that sustained pressure ushered him from the room and closed the door. Propelled thus on to the landing, Kemp put his back against the staircase railing. He felt in need of physical support; being small, he had an innate allergy to tall men standing over him.

There was a steady blue flame burning in Seft's eyes. With a sinking heart Kemp realized that it was not his intellect alone that had been working overtime during the last few minutes.

'Well, Kemp, this is how I see it. You brought my wife back here tonight. You tried to rape her—no, it's no use denying it—your prints are all over her shoes which you grabbed to pull her down. When she resisted you knocked her out, then you took her necklace. It's pretty immaterial whether you intended rape or theft or both...'

'Your wife won't go along with that cock-and-bull story. You were the one who hit her and she knows it.'

'You're mistaken, Kemp. Appearances can be deceptive. Don't put too much faith in all that quarrelsome stuff this evening. Judith and I understand one another. She'll do what I say. She loves me, you see.' It was said without arrogance; Seft was simply stating a fact as immutable as Boyle's Law, and it began to dawn on Kemp that it might be true.

'You've been married yourself,' Seft went on smoothly, 'so you'll know there's the most extraordinary loyalty. Through thick and thin, eh? Look what you did for your Muriel even though you knew she was rotten to the core...' Even as the words hit Kemp where it hurt and he resented their use by Seft, he had to give the man credit for his research. And he was right about Judith. Kemp had seen the evidence as they put her down on the bed, a double bed, his nightwear on one side, hers on the other. They shared that life. The whole evening's performance when she threw the force of her anger against him was just part of that possessive devouring love that will not let go. She would stand by her husband whatever he did.

Kemp sighed.

'I want to know where that necklace came from,' he said stubbornly.

'I'm sure you do. Judith must have seen your interest in it, and she'll know that's why you drove her home. She knows nothing about you but when she comes round I shall tell her exactly what you are. A scruffy little man of no value to anyone. And if you don't get out of our lives I'll make sure it's spread round this neighbourhood, starting with your friends the Plenders, that you attacked Judith tonight. It'll stick, Kemp, don't think it won't. You are a nobody. You are already a discredited nobody here in Leatown, and if you so much as put your dirty feet in any of our doors again I'll see to it that the charge is proved.'

He's overdoing it, thought Kemp, they always do, these self-made supermen. The more force in the re-action, the more Seft must have to hide. He knew himself no match for the doctor if it came to a trial of brute strength, but where mind met mind he knew his to be the sturdier since he had no secrets tucked away.

'I think Lucille Pearson had jewellery, including those emeralds in your wife's necklace,' he remarked conversationally, 'and if you're going to charge me with theft or rape, the police will be interested as to how they came into your wife's possession.'

Seft looked at him for a moment without speaking. The flame had died in his eyes, leaving them blue and cold as a winter sea.

'How does this strike you, Kemp,' he said at last, 'as to what really happened tonight? I came in only a short while ago. I found you standing over my wife with the necklace in your hand, and I shot you as any responsible husband and householder might do in the heat of the moment?'

A doctor who can produce a gun from his pocket as easily as he might bring out a stethoscope was a man of more than medical resource. Kemp had called his bluff and so drawn out the essence of him, steel-hard as the weapon in his hand.

'If you want another death,' said Kemp, trying to consider the word in the abstract while at the same time reassure his nerves that it had nothing to do with their present precarious circumstances, 'then that's a brisk enough solution, but you still have Malcolm Moss to deal with . . .'

Seft laughed, although the gun never wavered.

'You're pretty shrewd, Kemp. Don't worry, I'll get around to Moss in good time. I regularly visit my patients in Epping General—even in the middle of the night. That's where your call came from, didn't it? Poor blighter, he should have been dead by now . . .'

And if I can keep you here long enough, thought Kemp savagely, he won't even die hereafter. Frances Jessica. Would she be able to withstand this plausible fast-talker with the full exercise of medical privilege at his command? After all, it was only by a trick of his subconscious mind that Kemp himself had not succumbed to it. Askew had noticed. In the car as they followed the ambulance he had said: 'You called for an ambulance, Mr Lennox. Why not for the nearest doctor?' It hadn't struck Kemp until now. Was it because he had, almost without thinking, even then suspected Seft? Now he knew what it was that stopped him. An almost clairvoyant vision: of Angie Foster's body on that Forest road, the silly woolly cap and someone's arm raised above her defenceless head. And the doctor who had arrived so providentially—for who but a doctor can take an accident victim into hospital and have no questions asked?

'You're only playing for time, Kemp,' said Seft wearily, as if having made a snap diagnosis he was anxious to proceed with the operation.

An arrogant man. Judith had called him godlike, and in his profession that attitude could be given scope. Kemp wondered about his vanity; such men as Seft must all have vanity just as McCready thought their blood inherited.

'I admire you, Seft,' he said, 'I like self-made men and you've done well. Why not keep the jewels? They're worth a fortune—you must have seen that when Lucille showed them to you first. You can still get away with it. Her suicide's a *fait accompli*—it's in no one's interest to reopen that can of worms. As for the Foster girl—well, you can swing that one too, there'll be a verdict of misadventure. I suppose you heard her that time when she was delirious with 'flu—all about the green stones and the tall man. You thought she meant you, you thought Lucille had told her and paid her to keep quiet. You knew that kind of secret would never be safe with a girl like Angela. You and your precious Lucille . . .'

Benjamin Seft hadn't moved, he was simply watching Kemp run on as if his talk was gibberish. Kemp wanted his words to wound, to hurt Seft as deeply as he himself had been hurt by the unnecessary gibe at Muriel.

'You and Lucille . . . that's good for a laugh, eh? You and your maniac girlfriend—was it only the madness you had in common?'

For a split second Kemp thought he would be shot. Instead, Seft lunged at him furiously and as Kemp ducked, the gun smashed into the side of his head. As he fell, Kemp at least had the satisfaction of knowing why Seft had not fired; his violence was tempered by fear. Even as he tasted blood on his teeth, and hatred for the brutal, skin-splitting assault welled up inside him, Kemp forced out the words: 'Killing me will do you no good, Seft... I've already put them on to you... and there's been no inquest yet on Angela Foster...'

Ben Seft was down on the floor beside him, pressing the gun into the shattered flesh behind his ear. 'You're bluffing again, Kemp. There's nothing anybody can prove against me. Angela came off her bike and I found her. Doctors don't always have to save life, you know. She died of a fractured skull—what's another blow more or less?—it's still a fractured skull. She was a stupid girl. I'm always having to deal with stupid people. You're stupid too, Kemp, that's why you're going to die.'

Anger is more potent fuel to the nerves than courage. The cold rationality Seft brought to the murder of Angie roused in Kemp a primeval red rage he couldn't contain. He twisted and grabbed at the man's legs. The gun went off, a searing explosion deafened him, but as he brought Seft down the gun fell and skidded across the landing. A desperate lunge and Kemp had it. But even as he aimed, Seft scrambled to his feet and leapt for the stairs. Kemp could have shot him as he took a final jump into the hall but he stayed his hand. The wild surge of anger passed as quickly as it had come and a cold sense of reality supervened. He didn't want Seft dead. He might have tried to lame him but this was no time for target practice. Seft bounded across the hall like an animal and was out the front door by the time Kemp reached the foot of the stair. He heard the rattle of stones on the drive and, minutes later, the roar of the car.

Kemp put the gun in his pocket beside the necklace and went to have a look at Judith. Even the sound of the shot had not wakened her and she looked peaceful enough despite the dark bruise on her temple.

Kemp found the study and a telephone. There was a pad on the desk beside it with scribbled numbers—one was Epping General. Of course, that's what Seft would have done when he came back for the jewellery. Now he would be making a late call on a patient, and he would have told the night staff to expect him; he wouldn't need a gun there, medical practitioners had access to other lethal means if they had a mind to murder.

Kemp dialled. The blood from his ear dripped slowly on the orderly notes set out on the desk top; reports and records, statistics of bronchitis and asthma in Leatown, neat piles of letters and an open appointments diary—the paraphernalia of a health-saving, caring general practice. What mad aberration, what sinister motive had brought it all to nought? For Kemp was still not sure. Perhaps the answer lay with Malcolm Moss, and if so...

Kemp's breath was short by the time he got his call through.

'A patient...his wife is with him, a Mrs Moss... It's urgent I speak with her—tell her it's Mr Kemp...'

He waited for what seemed an eternity. But it wasn't her voice that spoke.

'Is that you, Lennox?'

He never expected to hear the Scotch voice with such gladness.

'McCready? What the devil...'

'Did you no' think I'd come myself? I got on to Comfrey like you said and he's with Moss now. The man's come round and he's talking. Doesn't make a lot of sense but I think you were right. Bad blood will out, like I always said. He's got a lot of explaining to do, your Malcolm Moss...'

'I wasn't right about him... Listen, McCready.'

It took a long time to convince him. Finally, Kemp said: 'So, if your police friends are at Moss's bedside, for God's sake keep them there and don't let anyone else in. And I mean anyone. I don't care if he's a doctor with a halo round his head. Oh, and send a constable round here...' He gave the address, then went in search of a bathroom and some towels to staunch the blood.

Gingerly dabbing at the wound, he sat in a chair in the hall and waited. If Seft saw the police cars at the hospital he might take warning, and return. He would be in a dangerous mood, there was no telling what harm he might do to the sleeping Judith. Kemp felt he owed her some protection; her ill-judged gesture tonight had brought its own retribution upon her but it had been of great help to Kemp.

When the constable arrived, not entirely clear as to his duties, Kemp told him very little beyond asking him to stay and be on hand to reassure Mrs Seft should she wake. There was a possibility grave charges might be laid against her husband; should he return, his attitude must govern how the policeman should deal with him.

As an afterthought, Kemp handed over Seft's gun. He tried to be a law-abiding citizen and he had no licence for it.

SEVENTEEN

DESPITE A PAINFUL throbbing behind his ear, Kemp
felt better outside in the cool air of the night. Patiently his little car had waited at the gate.

He drove off slowly in the direction of the Epping
Road. He did not feel capable of driving fast, and he
wanted time to think. If you go to court, he said to
himself, you are supposed to have all your facts in the
papers you bring, be prepared, and never leave your
wits at home. His wits kept trying to wander off and
he must get them gathered in for the approaching climax. He had no doubt that such a climax would come,
and come soon.

He turned off at Woodridden Hill to take the short
cut through St. Thomas' Quarters. There was a clear
moon sailing above hazy clouds, making black the
shadows and flooding the open spaces with white
light. Apart from the purring of the engine all was
peaceful, so that a drowsy calmness began to wash into
his mind cleansing it of the pressures of speculation—
an anodyne reflex against the too swift events of the
last few hours. The road ahead lay striped black and
white as the tall trunks took the moonlight, and the
undergrowth bushes moved behind the trees like wild

beasts prowling behind bars, just as there were tigers stalking the shadows in his tired, drifting mind.

One of the tigers leapt into reality. Kemp braked desperately as he caught the glint of the moon on red metal. You bloody fool, he swore to himself, you've let it happen again! The Morgan came out of the darkness of a lay-by on the left of the road and roared straight into his path. It struck his car on the bonnet, locked into it and both vehicles hurtled broadside into the bank where the Morris broke free and stopped, shivering but still upright. Kemp managed to wrench his door open, and he threw himself into the ditch as he saw Benjamin Seft scramble from his car where it had stuck half way up the grassy bank.

Kemp cursed the lawful instinct which had made him surrender that gun. It was not likely that the doctor would have had access to an armoury; nevertheless Kemp didn't fancy his chances with the big man should it come to a fight. Courage is relative to circumstances, and it might be that it would be better to throw valour to the winds and take to his heels, hoping his old knowledge of the Forest ways would be to his advantage. He hunched himself like a rabbit, and waited.

Seft was now slithering headlong down the bank behind his red car. Seeing Kemp, he paused for an instant, putting his hand momentarily on the rear of the vehicle to steady himself, then he came on, the moonlight making his face into a grimly smiling mask. So intent was he on reaching his quarry crouched below

him that he stumbled on a tree root, and fell. Kemp
watched with horror as the great car teetered and then
started to move slowly backwards. Before Seft could
rise it was on him, crashing down like a gigantic ham-
mer.

Kemp heard him scream, and the piercing sound
awakened the rooks in the tree-tops so that they flew
upwards in a scatter of rags.

Kemp ran over and knelt beside Seft. But there was
nothing he could do to shift that weight of metal pin-
ning the man fast into the soft leaf-mould of the forest floor.

IT WAS KEMP WHO got the morphine from the doctor's
case and filled the syringe, following the muttered
directions, but he was careful also to check the dos-
age, holding up the printed instructions to the benev-
olent moon. Just enough to kill the pain; he didn't
trust Ben Seft, even now. It would be Kemp's own
fingerprints on that syringe and he had no intention of
aiding and abetting a felony—no matter that it was for
a man already dying.

As he had leant in cautiously to remove the medical
bag from the rear seat of Seft's car, so he had also removed the dirty rolled-up canvas which lay beside it.
The time had come for all the jewels to be re-united.

'I'm going for help,' was all he could say to the
broken man beneath the car which had once belonged

to Leopold Pearson. Benjamin Seft barely nodded, then closed his eyes in acceptance.

Kemp set off to walk to the Epping Road where he waved down the first passing vehicle.

EIGHTEEN

BENJAMIN SEFT DID NOT die immediately. 'Not before he made a long statement,' Inspector Comfrey told Kemp and McCready early the next morning at Epping Police Station. 'Not that it was what you might call a confession, mind you,' he went on wryly. 'Oh, he knew he was dying all right—he'd a ruptured spleen and a lot of internal bleeding. He hadn't a chance and he knew it. It wasn't so much a statement as a record of his achievements.'

Kemp nodded. 'He was vain—like many of his kind. It's a pity, though, that he ended as he did. He'd come a long way. Did he tell you about his origins? They were supposed to be a dark secret.'

Comfrey snorted. 'That was just to make himself more interesting. Actually his family were respectable enough. His father had been unsuccessful in business, I gather, so there wasn't enough money for young Seft's medical training. I suppose that's what gave him the obsession with money and success. The mother seems to have had some kind of nervous breakdown—she died in a mental home...' Comfrey sighed. 'I sat by his bedside and took down his statement. He wanted everybody to know how clever he'd been.'

'If that car hadn't got him he might still have talked his way out. My death would have been the result of yet another accident—just a car crash in the Forest.'

'We'd have been hard pressed to prove any of your tale, Mr Kemp, if Seft hadn't talked,' Comfrey said.

'And he only talked because he was dying. He'd never have admitted anything otherwise. His power lay in checking up on other people's weaknesses and taking advantage of them.' Kemp looked across at McCready. 'Even you didn't believe me on the phone, did you?' McCready looked uncomfortable. 'I thought we'd got our man,' he said. 'Mrs Moss's idea about the suicide note seemed a bit thin—' he stopped and glared at Kemp—'and I didn't know what she was talking about because you had told me there was no note left by Moss. You lied to me about that!'

'I didn't,' Kemp said blandly, 'because it wasn't left by him, it was left by our doctor friend after he'd given Moss a shot in the arm. Maybe he tried to guide his hand when the man was drugged—whatever he did it was a clumsy attempt but it might just have served his purpose. Don't forget that Seft was the police doctor and a swift talker, he might well have overridden any objection by Mrs Moss that the note was not in her husband's hand. Told her that under the influence of whisky and sleeping tablets any man's writing changes . . . And it is in fact rather a scrawl.'

'Where is that note?' asked Comfrey sharply.

'At the moment it's a private communication ostensibly addressed to my client,' Kemp replied smoothly. 'When she has seen it I shall be happy to hand it over to you.' It was for Malcolm Moss himself to tell his wife what had been implied in the note, what Seft knew and used to authenticate the supposed suicide: that there had been a secret in Moss's life too terrible for him to bear. With this in mind, Kemp rounded on both McCready and Comfrey. 'You haven't told her who her husband is?'

They both shook their heads. 'But he can't keep it a secret any longer,' Comfrey said, 'And he's still got a lot of explaining to do, your Mr Malcolm Moss.'

'Will he be charged?'

Comfrey took up a sheet of paper.

'I've got a short statement here by Moss about how Seft met him out at that house last Monday night, got him down to the stable on the pretext that there was something there belonging to Lucille, and then gave him a jab in the arm. He says he doesn't remember much after that. What I can't understand is why Moss was fool enough to arrange to meet Seft at all—they didn't even know each other.'

'I think I know the answer to that. Moss got a letter from Brother Leopold still harping on the disappearance of the jewels. Leopold must have done a lot of thinking once he was safely across the sea. He had a good nose for a villain. I think he made some sly innuendoes in that letter about the eagerness of a certain doctor to give the evidence he did. Moss thought he could handle Seft. All he wanted to find out was how much Seft knew about him—and he'd have let him get away with the gems just to keep him quiet. But Seft had other plans. Moss's death by suicide would clear up the case nicely. We know now our late doctor was a meticulous man—he checked up on everyone he had to deal with. I bet he even looked up the wife's name in the electoral roll with the idea of concocting some last message... Of course he took the first one and got it wrong. But Moss himself never stood a chance that night he met Seft. You can imagine what happened. Lucille had already spilled the beans about who Malcolm Moss really was—Seft probably called him Ambrose to his face. That would be enough to send him reeling even before he was drugged.'

'Well, that's as may be.' Comfrey was not one given to speculation. 'The most we can charge Moss with—and I'm not saying we will when this complex matter has been properly investigated—is that he and his brother Leopold dumped their sister's body in the Wake Pond. He's admitted to that. Leopold gave false evidence at the inquest but it's not worth our police resources bothering about Pearson—he's a right rogue but he's no longer ours, thank God. They gave Malcolm Moss a bad time, these two.'

'Blackmail?' asked Kemp, and Comfrey nodded.

'Moss was a fool to let them get away with it, but all he wanted was a quiet life. Can't say I blame him in the circumstances. Imagine having something like that hanging over your head since you were a lad...' Kemp felt the Inspector's words to be more than apt.

'There was the smell of blackmail about the Moss affair from the first,' said Kemp, 'but I'd checked both of them, Malcolm Moss and his wife, pretty carefully and had found nothing but clean sheets...' He wondered too about his own choice of words, which set him thinking again of the golden bowl that had been so flawed from the start.

Comfrey cleared his throat. 'Well, the only illegal act he seems to have committed was helping to dispose of the body. It was clever of Seft to put it in the boot of that car. A stroke of genius, he called it...' Comfrey wiped his brow; listening to what Seft said as he lay dying had not been a pleasant experience. 'He killed her in the stable, you know—that's where they used to meet for whatever hanky-panky they were up to. She was serious enough about him—wanted him to go off to the States with her. All she had been waiting for was to get her hands on that jewellery. While the brothers were settling the score—we'll hear more about that from Moss himself when he's fit—Lucille had her own plans. She took the bag of jewellery and slipped away to meet Seft. She thought, I suppose, that the sight of the loot would convince him of his good fortune in getting her and enough riches to set them both up in the States. He was very, very nasty about Lucille...'

'I think I can guess what happened,' said Kemp. 'He laughed at her, she threatened him, she probably went hysterical—he hates neurotic women—and he killed her. How?'

'We'll never know for certain. He says he put his hands to her throat to quieten her—he's a strong man.'

'H'm.' McCready looked sceptical. 'I think he saw a great opportunity and took it. He was a cool one, though, he must have thought himself in luck when the death was never reported.'

'Lucille told Seft quite a lot about the game she and Leopold had going with Moss. Seft knew Leopold couldn't afford a police investigation into the death of his sister, and of course later they both backed each other up at the inquest. What really worried Seft was the Foster girl—he didn't know just how much Lucille had gabbled to her about the stones. He didn't care about being suspected of having an affair with Lucille—that could all be hushed up—but at some time in the future he had to realize the value of that jewellery. Angela Foster was the only one to whom Lucille could have shown it—if she ever did.' Comfrey stopped, and took up the canvas bag from his desk. He poured the contents out, a pool of sparkling colour, brilliant and unforgiving.

'From the records of the Ambrose case that's at least half the spoils of the Hatton Garden job,' said McCready.

Kemp kept his mouth shut. There was still one stone in Joseph Crohn's safe.

'They're what Benjamin Seft killed for,' said Comfrey, getting up. 'Aye, and what he died for. It's been a long night, and I've got a lot of work still to do. I'll need a statement from you, Mr Kemp, but you don't look in very good shape at the moment. It can wait.'

'I'll run you home, laddie,' said McCready as they left the station. 'Your car's still stuck back on yon road in the Forest anyway.'

It cleared Kemp's mind, talking to McCready on their way back to London. Besides, it gave him a certain satisfaction to have blown a hole in the older man's precious theory.

'I'll grant you Moss has been a fool but he's no worse,' he told McCready, 'and you wonder why he didn't go to the police? Just remember, his father was hanged for killing a policeman. He's got the body of a strangled woman in his car, and she's his sister. He doesn't know who killed her, he's being blackmailed, he's been trying for years to protect his wife from the knowledge that she's married to the son of a murderer—oh no, Malcolm Moss would never go to the police!'

'How did you find out he was another son of the Ambroses?' McCready asked.

'I was curious about Moss right from the beginning. He seemed to be too good to be true. Then when I did some research on the Ambrose case I found a discrepancy. It was in an obscure provincial paper—some reporter trying to get the reactions of neighbours to the Ambrose family when they had lived in Birkenhead some years before. A woman interviewed said they'd kept themselves to themselves and all she had seen was the little boy going past her gate on his

way to school. Well, Leopold was only five when
Leonie Ambrose took him and the baby Lucille off to
the States so he wouldn't have been going to school a
few years earlier. There must have been another child.
Malcolm Moss began his architectural training in
Liverpool and his matriculation was from Birkenhead Institute. Then when I'd seen the newspaper
pictures of Lawrence Ambrose, I was certain. There's
a strong family likeness, the long face and the eyes…'

The face of the Harp girl came back into Kemp's
mind; he had been puzzled the first time he met Moss
by something familiar. Lucille, too, had looked like
her father.

Back at his flat Kemp had a wincing hot bath, re-
paired as well as he could the damage to his broken
skin, and decided before taking a well-earned rest that
he would contact his solicitor.

Tony Egerton gave him a cautious 'hello.'

'I would like you to call off my proposed purchase
of Green Acres,' said Kemp, very businesslike.

'I thought you would somehow,' Tony said. 'Can I
give them a reason?'

'I don't think they're going to need one. Mr Askew
of Benson's will quite understand. I've no wish to buy
a property that gets strewn with bodies,' said Kemp
primly.

Tony chuckled.

'Come off it, Lennox, that's right up your street.'
Then he became serious. 'There's a lot of rumours in
Leatown this morning. Know anything about them?'

'You know me, Tony. I don't deal in rumours. Just call off the purchase, there's a good chap. Oh, and send me your bill.'

'Don't be daft. Well, I suppose we'll get an official communiqué in due course but this place is fairly rattling with skeletons already. You certainly have a nose for trouble. Anything else I can do for you?'

'There is one thing. Give me a brief rundown on *donatio mortis causa*. It's so long since I practised law that I forget things.'

'Give me the circumstances.'

Kemp told him an expurgated version. There was a pause.

'Not a snowball's chance in hell.'

'Ah well, it was worth trying. Thanks, Tony.'

I'll sell it to old Crohn, thought Kemp dispassionately, Violet and that family of hers could do with a windfall. The death of Angie still weighed heavily on Kemp's conscience. If only he had picked up the pieces more quickly, if only, if only... He fell asleep.

NINETEEN

THE CALL CAME IN the late afternoon. Kemp struggled up out of dreamless depths, and heard her voice.

'He wants to see you. He wants to thank you.'

'I don't think . . . I don't want to see him . . .'

Kemp stared at his curtained windows, seeing the dazzle of sunlight through the pattern. He couldn't explain his reluctance. He felt himself pushing against the appeal she was making, he only wanted to thrust her out of his thoughts, out of his life.

'Please,' she said again.

So of course he went.

MALCOLM MOSS SITTING up in his hospital bed in hard-laundered patients' pyjamas was not the same man who had strode so belligerently about Kemp's flat sneering at the furniture.

Kemp took the hand held out to him, and sat down. The fingers had been clammy yet left his own feeling chilled. He wondered if, in the light of what he now knew, he could still maintain his dislike.

'The only thing that concerns me now, Mr Kemp, is how much does my wife have to know?'

Kemp would give him no comfort on that score.

'She will have to know it all. It'll be in the Press. Besides you haven't done anything wrong. She'll understand.'

'*You* don't understand, Mr Kemp. No one can.'

The crêpey lids came down briefly over the hollowed eyes.

'I'll try and explain,' said Malcolm Moss, 'but words won't be easy. They never were. People don't talk about such things. Aunt Moss and her husband—she was my mother's aunt, Clara Moss—they weren't articulate and anyway the situation was too terrible to talk about... My mother left me with them because she was afraid I'd give her away in her new life. I've never felt bitter about that—it seemed then and still does to have been plain good sense. I never felt deprived or ill-used because of it. Clara Moss saw to that. She gave me not only a home but something else—the moral certitude of pure goodness. Do you believe in absolute goodness, Mr Kemp?'

Kemp shook his head. 'I don't deal in absolutes,' he said, 'only with people.'

'People are rarely absolutes,' said Moss, 'but Clara Moss did have the quality of absolute goodness. In that little bare house in a backstreet she taught me how to be good. And I knew it was the only path I could take—there could be no half-measures for me with my history. Oh, I heard plenty of talk about the Ambrose case outside that house. I soon learned what my mother was and what my father had done. There was only one way I could go, and instinctively—for she wasn't a clever woman and she knew nothing about psychology—Clara Moss set my feet on that strict road.'

He stopped, and Kemp silently handed him a glass of water.

'At first, school was hell,' Moss went on, his troubled eyes reflective, 'until one day a big boy cornered me in the playground and jeered: "You're Ambrose whose father was hung for killing a cop." I said no, I wasn't. I was Malcolm Moss and I lived at thirty-two Greenfield Street with my mother and father. I saw he believed me, and I learnt the power of lies. I became Malcolm Moss and I never used the name Ambrose again. Clara helped—they adopted me. They were my parents. John Moss died of TB—he'd never been strong since that other war—and she lived her life out in that same house. I tried to repay her but she didn't care about money. Of my life up till ten she never spoke—neither did I—it had long been pushed from my memory. To Clara Moss I was a child who had been brushed by evil, a brand to be saved from the burning. She saw to it that I knew the difference between good and bad—she never acknowledged any grey areas in between. She taught me a strict code, and as I grew older I knew why she had done it. I was never to cheat, not even in small ways, never be tempted to take short cuts to money, never to swear or be angry, or have violent feelings towards anyone. Do I sound a prig?'

Kemp said nothing, and Moss gave a twisted smile.

'Clara Moss made me good. I didn't say she made me likeable. It wasn't easy...the instincts are there... And when I said the memory of my real parents faded, that isn't strictly true. I lived with the picture of that scene at the prison every day of my life. No one can understand what it was like...' Moss's voice had weakened. Then it was firm again as he said: 'I was fortunate—I met and married Jessica, a good woman, like Clara Moss. You may smile, Mr Kemp, but goodness is something you only recognize if you've known the other side intimately. I recognized it in Jessica. But our marriage had to be different. I had never made close friends, I suppose I'm not a very companionable person. Jessica seemed to accept it, she's an exceptional woman. I think we were happy... Then at the end of last year the others came...'

For the first time there was bitterness in his voice.

'They arrived like birds of prey. I had bought that land at High Beech to build a house for Jessica and myself, it was to be a surprise for her. My firm was doing well. Leopold had me traced. They'd run through their fortune in the States—they were out for plunder. He wanted the house and money, all she wanted was the jewellery. Unless I handed over everything to them they'd tell Jessica that I was the son of a murderer and a thief, that my brother was a con-man and my sister a crazy degenerate—for that's what Lucille was. She was more dangerous than him—she'd stop at nothing. Playing that game the awful evening when she came for me just one of her little sadistic ideas. But they were both evil. Brother and sister of mine they were not. They were everything I'd been brought up to loathe. I would have done anything to get rid of them.'

'Even murder?'

Malcolm Moss gave Kemp a long slow look.

'Don't imagine I didn't think of it—I had to fight my genes as well. But no, the code of behaviour instilled into me by Clara Moss would not let me take that course. But I would fight for my marriage—and pay any price. You, Mr Kemp, were aware of that.'

Kemp acknowledged it; much of the steely quality which Moss had brought to his flat that night was still apparent, despite the man's obvious sickness.

Moss sipped some water.

'It was the jewellery that did it. When I was twenty-one Clara Moss gave me the canvas bag, and told me that it had been left by my mother for them to use. It had lain unopened, untouched. To Clara it was filth. Even in the bad days when her husband was ill and she had to go out cleaning to keep us, she never went near the bag that contained a fortune. But she had promised Leonie Ambrose to give me the jewels if there were any left when I grew up, and she did. I also put it away. What would you have had me do? If I took it to the police it would all come out, who I was and who my father was. So I put the bag away, but years later I used to have the odd stone set for Jessica on her birthdays. It was wrong, I knew, but I couldn't resist . . .'

'Lucille took the jewels as her share of the blackmail?'

'She was like a child with them. She spread them out on the floor and danced round them. Of course when she and Leopold descended on me they never thought the jewels would still be intact. I suppose their mother had told them about the other half of the stolen stuff but they never expected to see the jewels. They had wanted money, and they'd have gone on wanting money, but I knew the jewels would get rid of them, they would have to go back to the States to sell them. I convinced them that Scotland Yard still had records of the stones—I didn't know whether it was true or not but it did the trick once Lucille had seen them. That week in May Leopold forced me to stay out there until my cheques were cleared—I suppose he didn't trust me. You know, of course, that I sold part of my business to raise the money, and he had some nefarious scheme to get the currency out of the country. Everything was cleared up that Friday night, and he let me go . . .'

'About half past nine?'

Malcolm Moss leaned back on his pillows.

'Are you all right? Don't go on. I know the rest.'

'It was a nightmare. I thought I was in the clear, they'd be gone the next day. Lucille said she was going down to the stable to say goodbye to her pony. When

I looked into that half-open boot, the body was still warm. I panicked, and let Leopold take charge ...'

'I think I have tired you.' Kemp rose to go.

Malcolm Moss put out his hand once more.

'I'm sorry. I've been far too full of myself. And I've not thanked you. The Inspector has told me something of your part in all this—your tenacity, as he called it. I was so involved with the past, my own past, that I wasn't thinking straight about the killing of Lucille. All I wanted was to keep myself out of trouble—I never thought of justice in connection with the death, and I should have done. Even when I got that letter from Leopold about Dr Seft I was still only concerned for myself. I had to find out if he knew about me ... My life has made me very self-centered, I'm afraid ...'

'You were only protecting your own—most of us do it all the time. I've stayed long enough. And your wife will be waiting to come in...' Kemp hesitated. He was not altogether sure of his ground. 'I shouldn't worry about her knowing the truth. I think you married a better woman than you know, and you won't find her any different. She's not the changing kind.'

KEMP HAD HIS last meeting with Frances Jessica Moss in the hospital waiting-room—that wearisome place of lost footfalls. They sat together in a corner on a hard bench.

'You've known for some time, haven't you?' he said to her.

Her light brown eyes were placid.

'Oh yes, I've always known who Malcolm was.'

This extraordinary woman never ceased to surprise him.

'You mean since you married?'

'Lennox,' she said, 'my mother may have had little money, but she was a gentlewoman and I was her only daughter. She was naturally interested in the man I chose to marry. She had connections—it was all done very unobtrusively, but, yes, we both knew he was Malcolm Ambrose.'

Kemp stared at her. 'And she let you marry him?'

She smiled. 'She liked what she saw in him, as I did, and she had no prejudices. Malcolm was, and always will be, a good man. And of course she was absolutely right—I have the happiest of marriages.'

'But you never told him you knew?'

'We each kept our secret. Would you have had him know that I knew so that every time there was a murder in the papers or there was a debate about the return of capital punishment he would be afraid to meet my eyes? No, Lennox, until the time came for him to tell me himself I would wait.'

Kemp had to say it. He had spoken roughly to her before, and now he didn't spare her.

'So all this need never have happened. There was nothing for him to be blackmailed about! You knew who Lucille was that night she came...'

Her eyes clouded and faint rose coloured her cheeks.

'I guessed. She looked like him. I thought they might harm him. That was why I came to you . . .'

'God protect us from the simplicity of the good!' The words burst from Kemp before he could snatch them back, but she was not to be shaken.

'You must take people as you find them, Lennox.' After a pause while he considered the implications of such an all-embracing statement, she asked him: 'When did you guess that I knew about Malcolm's past?'

'Well, not when you made the remark—' Kemp was thinking back, as he did all too often for his peace of mind, to that sunny afternoon among the roses—'we had been talking about Madame Bovary. You said the saddest thing in the book was in one of the last paragraphs. I looked it up. The little girl whom nobody bothered about—she had to go out and work in a cotton-mill, didn't she? Just a throwaway line in a book and I kept wondering why you'd noticed it. You were thinking about another child, Malcolm Ambrose . . .'

She stood up and gave him her hand, still smiling. It was a gesture almost willing him to kiss it, so secure was she in her unassailable virtue. Kemp held it for a brief moment, then released it and strode out through the door in pettish bad temper.

Frances Jessica Moss went in to her husband.

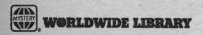

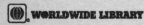

Can you keep a secret?

You can keep this one plus 2 free novels.

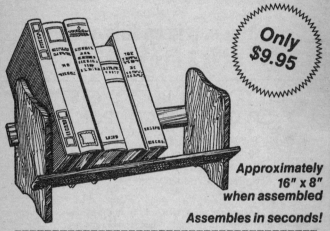